Praise for
THE LOVERS

Shortlisted for the 2023 Miles Franklin Literary Award
Shortlisted for the 2023 Victorian Premier's Literary Award for Fiction

'Her writing is poetic and reverential. The author's understanding of love, romance and of responsibility runs deep.' —*Books+Publishing*

'Sometimes, Kassab shows us, love can be another word for cruelty. Sometimes the stories we hide behind reveal our deepest truths.' —*Sydney Morning Herald*

'Beautifully told in Yumna Kassab's poetic prose, *The Lovers* is both the story of the tumultuous relationship between Amir and Jamila and an exploration of class, culture and the complex nature of love.' —*Sunday Life*

'A raw, haunting and honest look at love, relationships, and the moments that break us.' —*Mamamia*

'In she draws us, around her hearth, with the wise, suspenseful lilt of a tale well told.' —*Kill Your Darlings*

'The delicate power that fables hold – their universality, while retaining their specificity – is captured in *The Lovers*. Ultimately, Kassab's novel rests on the premise of the "impossibility of language, of being able to ever understand someone else."' —*Artshub*

Praise for
AUSTRALIANA

Shortlisted for the 2022 University of Queensland Fiction Book Award

'The real deal.' —Favel Parrett, author of *Past the Shallows* and *There Was Still Love*

'Kassab creates an eerie sense of place as the reader is drawn into myriad perspectives and geographies. Without doubt *Australiana* is an unnerving contribution to contemporary novel writing in this continent.' —*Books+Publishing*

'poetic, wise and peppered with black humour' —*T: The New York Times Style Magazine Australia*

'It is a novel of themes, textures, and interplay, seeking engagement through white space and chorus.' —*The Australian*

'There are times that reading these stories feels like being let in on some juicy gossip. And other times, we witness tragedy that is usually hidden from outsiders. In this way, I see *Australiana* as not merely challenging the established mythology of the regions but creating a new one.' —*Sydney Review of Books*

'*Australiana* plays with myths of Australian bush life while simultaneously restoring focus on the stories of those who live their lives in the regions. I recognise my young self and those I lived among in its pages.' —*The Conversation*

POLITICA

ALSO BY YUMNA KASSAB

The House of Youssef
Australiana
The Lovers

POLITICA

YUMNA KASSAB

The stories 'The Mountain', 'The Beggar' and 'Juggling' have been previously published in *The Saturday Paper*.

Published in 2024 by Ultimo Press,
an imprint of Hardie Grant Publishing

Ultimo Press
Gadigal Country
7, 45 Jones Street
Ultimo, NSW 2007
ultimopress.com.au

   ultimopress

All rights reserved. No part of this publication may be reproduced, stored in a retrieval system or transmitted in any form by any means, electronic, mechanical, photocopying, recording or otherwise, without the prior written permission of the publishers and copyright holders.

The moral rights of the author have been asserted.

Copyright © Yumna Kassab 2024

 A catalogue record for this book is available from the National Library of Australia

Politica
ISBN 978 1 76115 200 9 (paperback)

Cover design and illustrations Mika Tabata
Author photograph Courtesy of Tiger Webb
Text design Simon Paterson, Bookhouse, Sydney
Typesetting Bookhouse, Sydney | 11.75/17.75 pt Linotype Sabon Pro
Copyeditor Camha Pham
Proofreader Rebecca Hamilton

10 9 8 7 6 5 4 3 2

Printed in Australia by Opus Group Pty Ltd, an Accredited ISO AS/NZS 14001 Environmental Management System printer.

MIX
Paper | Supporting responsible forestry
FSC® C018684

The paper this book is printed on is certified against the Forest Stewardship Council® Standards. Griffin Press – a member of the Opus Group – holds chain of custody certification SCS-COC-001185. FSC® promotes environmentally responsible, socially beneficial and economically viable management of the world's forests.

Ultimo Press acknowledges the Traditional Owners of the Country on which we work, the Gadigal People of the Eora Nation and the Wurundjeri People of the Kulin Nation, and recognises their continuing connection to the land, waters and culture. We pay our respects to their Elders past and present.

FOR MY FATHER

The personal is political.
—*Anonymous*

CONTENTS

JAMAL   1

POLITICA   21

THE WELL   69

1973   115

HISTORIA   171

THE LINE ABOUT THE EAST

What did school matter when there was a war going on?

His father told Jamal to eat his food and to make sure he attended school. *So there are ideas to feed your head. Otherwise we will make the same mistakes over and over, like the souls trapped in the East.*

Jamal was not sure where this East was but he knew it was somewhere beyond the troubles of his life.

And what were the troubles of his life?

He was young and the army saw no need for him.

People were dying every day for their ideas and he walked to school daily because his father made him and he could not get his father to see his point no matter how much they argued over ideas.

Let me join a group. I can be useful. I can carry a gun.

His father stopped ruffling his hair and Jamal knew his dad was restraining himself.

Some ideas are worth fighting for but very few of them are worth your life.

His father used this line and it killed off their conversation each time. Jamal tried to come up with a response but all his answers died and for now his father won each round of this argument they had.

He knew he should go to school for now until he understood this reference to the East and then one day Jamal would be able to formulate an argument that'd silence his father so that his life could be his own and properly begin.

THE BEAR WITH A SORE HEAD

His father is dying. He has taken to his bed and he is waiting for his end. 'Don't worry about doctors and hospitals. I want to die here in my home.'

Jamal holds his father's hand because it seems to be the thing to do.

His father snatches his hand back. 'I'm dying but it's not my time yet. Go get me some tea.'

He makes the tea, he pours them each a cup, he wonders how long till his mother returns from the markets, how long he will be alone with his father's demands.

'Are you comfortable?'

'Am I comfortable?' his father roars. 'Am I comfortable? I'm dying and you ask me if I'm comfortable?'

Jamal stares at the ceiling and waits for his father to calm. It takes a while. His father mutters through his tea, he screams when he is asked a question he doesn't like.

'I would banish you to Siberia if I could.'

Later Jamal looks up Siberia in the atlas. It is far away and what Jamal wants to know is if Siberia is a country or a region. He checks the other pages, he checks the other books, but he cannot figure it out and meanwhile the person who knows the answer will explode and shut down all conversation because they're treating him like the already dead.

Jamal thinks to ask a teacher, a professor one day. He stores this question at the back of his mind and waits for a future when he can ask his question without having to deal with his father's rage.

REVOLUTION AND RAGE

Was this the revolution?

Jamal watched the men eating out of cans, their faces turned to the TV or the radio held by those at the fringe.

It was calm, very calm.

There were no guns allowed in a civilian place so only the smaller ones were kept here as the men relaxed.

There was a card game. It looked like 400.

There was a group doing their prayers and as soon as they finished another group began. The prayer corner was rarely unoccupied these days and the same could be said for this house.

It was Abdullah's house and there was talk about Abdullah's whereabouts but they were all rumours and remained unconfirmed.

Soon he would return.

Soon he would and then there he was.

Abdullah was one of the early figures. He was a legend but if you reached out, you knew him to be flesh and blood.

Jamal had spoken to Abdullah the very first day. He had called him sir and later realised no one addressed him like that but the men who heard him did not laugh.

His first night, he lay awake thinking about them laughing behind his back but the next day he could not find evidence for this sense and he gradually abandoned the idea and realised he was considered one of the men.

The men passed him bread, they passed him meat, they asked him to be on their team in cards, they nudged him when they went to pray. The men took their time to show him how to shoot, how to roll a cigarette. His father was going to stomp the life out of him for smoking. That is if he ever made it home again.

Abdullah sat in the seat that was unofficially his, that was kept vacant even if the men had to sit on the floor. He always looked clean no matter how dirty the day had been. Jamal pointed this out to someone and the response was *just because we're fighters doesn't mean we live like pigs.*

Abdullah with his neat beard, Abdullah with his shirt tucked in.

'We have lost many men today. There will be funerals but no tit for tat just to make sure we see an equal number of them dead. We'll go visit the families and make sure that they get the help they need. Keep your weapons close in case some see this as a suitable time to attack. There will be people who wish to join our cause. Remember, this is not a matter of numbers but about having people we can trust with our lives.'

Abdullah looked down at his plate as someone asked the names of the men.

'Abdul-Razak, Hamza, Ahmed Zein, Tariq ibn Ezedinne.'

They were silent and ate quietly. Some men left. Some prayed. Some continued with the game of cards.

Later, Jamal considered this the greatest lesson of his life.

Rage could be quiet. Rage could be the scream kept inside.

Rage could be patience as they buried their dead and went about their lives.

A MARTYR

When the news came about Suzan and the truck and the building and the dead, Jamal and the men cleared out because Abdullah was in a rage.

The internal story differed to the official story but both versions had holes.

Abdullah lined them up as if before a firing squad and demanded they speak.

Who supplied the truck?
Who supplied the bombs?
Who supplied the idea?
How many of you were in on this?
The location, its choice, the time of day?
How did you decide she'd be the one to drive the truck?

Ahmed spoke quietly. 'She volunteered. It was an idea we discussed but nothing had been decided. I was involved, there were others, and I suppose we believed this way we could make a point to the world.'

'And what point is that? That her life is worthless enough to throw away in this way?'

'It is not like that.'

'Then how is it? Explain it to me so I understand.'

'They can kill us just as well. What difference does it make? They are more powerful but we can make a point that we are not afraid, that we will persist with this even at the cost of our own lives. We are not afraid, Abdullah, we are not afraid. Do you understand?'

'But I am. We fight for this and in the end we kill ourselves as easily as they kill us. Why the fight if there is no one left?'

Abdullah turned from them and they avoided looking in his direction, they avoided thinking about the end of Suzan's life, if she had maintained her certainty or if there had been a moment, the impending afterlife, the Creator, and she had been afraid?

'We will not turn her into a martyr,' Abdullah said, but their minds were already someplace else.

'It is beyond our hands, Abdullah.' Ahmed said it and Jamal was afraid how this would affect their cause and their lives. 'This tide is beyond us. You think to direct it but it is outside our control. How she is seen is not for you and me to decide. There are forces greater than us at play here. If she is not made into a hero, she will have wasted her life. Do you understand?'

Abdullah was about to cry. They could see he was shaking, that his control was fragile, and Jamal left with the others, thinking today there will be a funeral, there will be a parade and Suzan will stare at them from the buildings, a rare smile or else her signature frown.

EQUALITY

'No, I don't wish to play nice, I don't wish to play fair. Did they ever play fair? Why then do you tell me I have to be fairer than them? I don't want to, I refuse to, and I wish you would stop telling me to.

'What I wish is to retaliate! I wish to hurt them how I have been hurt. I want it to be exact, the precise amount I have suffered.

'You tell me to walk away but I am in the mood for a fight, I am in the mood to chase after them. The better person walks away. The better person knows when to stay, when to leave, but you have made an assumption about me and what I believe. You assume I want to be better than them but the truth is I want to be as bad as them, and on a bad day I want to be worse.'

HERE IS THE ENEMY

It is Abu Rashid and they have captured him. Here he is in fact and Jamal thinks he is in control, that he is calm, but he can't hear a thing and it takes him a while to realise Munthir is calling his name.

'We should take him in.'

Take him in? Where? What does it mean to *take him in*? Do they take him as a prisoner, as a specimen alive or dead? He is worth more alive and Abdullah has repeatedly emphasised this. *We do not kill. We are not killers. We will be answerable for how we act.*

No words of Abdullah, no threat of God is going to keep him from Abu Rashid.

He wishes to destroy him but he does not know where to begin.

He lunges at Abu Rashid. Munthir grabs for his arm and drags him back. Munthir slaps his head, his arm, his back, but still he sees only Abu Rashid.

This is a dirty business. We don't want to end up dirtier still.

His father? Abdullah? Someone else?

Abu Rashid has his eyes closed but then opens them and looks directly at Jamal as if Munthir does not exist.

'If you are going to kill me, go ahead and do it so we can both be in peace.'

Jamal throws a bottle at him and it hits Abu Rashid in the chest. 'It is not for you to decide, it is not for you to order me.'

Munthir shakes him. 'Come on. This is embarrassing.'

Jamal pushes Munthir, he grabs his gun, he stares at Abu Rashid who refuses to open his eyes again.

He imagines it. He will shake him, he will kick, he will spit, he will tear his head from his body, he will, he will, he will do no such thing.

Munthir takes out a cigarette and lights it and asks Abu Rashid if he smokes. A shake of his head and so Munthir smokes alone.

Jamal knows the moment is over, that Munthir is in control, that his chance has disappeared, so he walks outside and looks at the sky and cries over the uselessness of tears to change the course of the world.

THINGS ABDULLAH SAID

'You need to go home. You're a mess. You're a useless fighter to everyone in this state.'

'Some people fall in love with revolutions and they fall in love with violence. Once the revolution was navigating from A to B, we arrive, we have no need for our guns but some become enraptured by carrying guns. They want to always carry them and they have no need for a life without violence. This is a sickness that traps everyone and I want no confusion over the purpose of our fight. This is our destination. Once we get there, the purpose is to resume our lives. I have a child, I have my wife, and I do not wish to be a human being who only finds meaning in a fight.'

'I wish to teach you as I wish to teach my child. We are alive, there is the sun outside. I do not wish to trivialise the value or meaning of a human's life whether on our side or on theirs.'

'Will my child one day lead my men? Who knows what waits for us, where we will find our end! The people who ask this forget my child is young, she has her own future, one day she will decide what she wishes to do with herself.'

'It is not all about swords, it is not all about guns. There is always a place in this for restraint. At the end of the day, the world suffers if we cannot sit at tables and actually talk.'

ONE LAST TIME

Later his father is dying, later his father has died. He wants to grab his father's body before it is buried in the grave. He wants to stop them, he wants to tell them he is not done, that only yesterday their conversation was interrupted, that he still has things to say.

He stands there quietly, he looks down to where his father lies and to his mind comes the line he has heard each time someone has died. *We are all on the same road.* Lately it is a line he has heard often and it could be that he knows many people or it could be that death has been busier as of late. It could be either of those but his father is dead and his body is coming to its final home. He tries to remember their conversation and his only memory is that it stopped, that its end remained undone. He searches, he casts his mind, he reaches out, he struggles for words, for other details that will bring about the conversation's return but it eludes him and it keeps him up at night. He counts the days at first as if to prove he has failed over a fundamental fact and perhaps it is a failure to leave the business of life undone: the conversation incomplete. His father's day is done, his end has come about, and his mind is on a memory from when he was seven.

He arrived home from school distressed. Mohammed had turned the other boys on him and he no longer had any friends. His father gave him half an orange, then half an apple, he gave him half of whatever fruit he ate. *You will find a way to live with him.* And his father's words, he accepted them for they had the weight of God's, and his understanding was his father was saying that he and Mohammed should be friends. Well, Mohammed was mean and the next day Mohammed hit him again, and when he arrived home, he threw his bag so that it hit the chairs. There was no fruit this time but his father told him to wash his face. 'I have washed my face and so what?' His father asked him what happened and he shouted, 'You're the one who told me to be his friend!' His father slapped him and he began to cry all over again.

Now he hears his father in his ear as he lies awake and he wants to take him from his grave and demand that he explain himself, that he explain what he meant. *I did not tell you to befriend him, I did not tell you to pretend. I said you will learn to live with him. You avoid him, you find other friends, do not be afraid if you need to hit him back, but Mohammed is not your kind and he is not the only person in the world.*

He thinks of the revolution, the fighting without end, the Mohammeds he has encountered in his life, the Mohammeds he knew to be enemies from the start, the Mohammeds that later show their true face and it is a betrayal that hurts him every single time. This is the conversation that remains, this is the conversation that is undone, that possesses him, and really he is going to take a shovel in this darkness and dig the bastard up and shake him till he is given a response that makes sense, that gives him an end in sight. But there will be no answer, there will never be another answer.

All he knows is that his father is gone and he will never say another word to him again in this life. And perhaps he finds the answer in this life or, as he now believes, it is increasingly likely that he will not.

It is a tale
Told by an idiot, full of sound and fury,
Signifying nothing.
—*Macbeth*

THE HANDSHAKE

Yasmeen, Yasmeen, the world calls to you to take the stage on this appointed hour. Yasmeen, Yasmeen, we have agreed and we have gone through this a hundred times. There is the stage, there are the cameras. When the clock reaches twelve, you will step out, you will walk to the centre of the stage and you will meet him there, and the world will clap. You will stand there, he will stand at your side and you will reach for each other's hands. A shake, the cameras, the President smiling on. As we agreed. As we signed. As the world holds its breath. Yasmeen, Yasmeen, do you understand?

She holds her head in her hands.
    She agreed but she was not meant to have agreed.
    She agreed but she has made an awful mistake.
    She agreed but there is no agreement.
    She holds her head and she thinks: the thousands killed, the others displaced, the scattering, the binding, the people who disappeared and were never seen again, others imprisoned and he will not hand them to her, the homes destroyed, the children with death in their eyes.

And she has agreed to peace with this man. They sold out their hopes for a stage and a photograph. The handshake. It shall fall at the appointed hour. She rehearsed it with him before the empty seats. She sold out the dead for the sake of a false dream.

She holds her head and she thinks: it was not meant to be like this.

Yasmeen, Yasmeen, you were brought here because you want peace. We want peace as you want peace. Why else have we fought all these years? This thing you want, we will give it to you, and all you have to do is agree and shake his hand. For your peace, you agree to raise no weapons, to cease your fight, to educate your young about this darkness and how we meant you peace all along. For this promise, you will sign, you will shake his hand, and then it will be peace as you so long wished.

She can hear them. Cameras, the babble of voices, the announcer calling her name. She shuts her eyes. She pictures them waiting for her. In rehearsals, she was the last to join the stage. The President smiled on.

She stands, she draws her scarf tight around her neck and steps out to the world waiting below.

They watch, they hold their breath, they call her name.

He waits, his head turns to her but not his body. His body was meant to be turned to her. It was meant to be the signal: *agreement, unity, we are together for harmony.* Except he faces the crowd, only an eye is turned her way.

She reaches him. The President nods to her and she is sick but she steadies herself. Her enemy, her opponent, the one she swore to fight all her years, he waits for her to hold out her hand. As they agreed, as they signed, as they rehearsed.

He waits.

She does nothing.

The President stares her down.

The crowd is uncertain.

He holds out his hand.

She does not meet him midair.

She means to speak, she means to say: *I will not participate in my annihilation.* She means to say it, she thinks it, but the sentence remains silent in her mind.

She feels the bullet and she falls to her knees.

She looks up and he stares her down.

The President watches on.

The crowd is silent.

She shuts her eyes and she thinks: they will have their peace. It was arranged in her presence but they can easily have it without.

POLITICA

They met at university, students born in the same year. Khadija was born in May, and Abdullah's birthday followed thirty days after in the middle of June. They were enrolled in the subject *Introductory Politics*, an overview of the events that shaped their present world.

It is a dry subject, he whispered.

I expected more intrigue was her response.

He ran into her on campus, they argued over their favourite books. When he told her he meant to bring freedom to their people, she shrugged and opened her book. She proceeded to write a four-thousand-word essay on the history of their nation and why their people would never be free. When she was done, she tapped him on the arm and said, 'I have written something you need to read. I'll make a copy and give it to you next week.'

He read her words and everything she wrote was true but he would not stand for it and so he wrote a rebuttal to her every point, typing it carefully and handing it to her the next time they met. 'Your essay is well written but here is why I do not think it will end up being true.'

Those two essays were references in the first weeks of their friendship. They spoke of them often as another couple might laugh over a private joke. She reminded him of his choice of words when they argued, he threw her words at her whenever they disagreed. Those troubles were a private matter and in public they wore the smile of marital unity, never revealing their hidden discord.

When he started the movement, when he became the voice of a cause, she often thought back to their university days. She imagined alternatives: she had not written the essay, he had not bothered to read it, he had accidentally left it on a bus. Had she not written it, perhaps their lives would have taken a different course.

In the days after his death, she thought of their first coffee, their first dinner, their first argument more and more. As her daughter hid in her room and her grandson was left to supervise himself, she thought of other essays she could have written. There was love and botany and navigating by the stars. Instead their world had been an endless conversation of politics and in the end it took his life and its price would be her daughter too. These hypotheticals are a dark bucket and whatever she fishes out is not worth the effort so she may as well find her grandson and teach him to dream anew.

A NAME OF FLOWERS

She had a baby girl.

Years he has dreamed of this day and here it is.

Khadija hands him their daughter. They agreed her name shall be Yasmeen. At last a child, both of them had given up all hope. It is a year since that argument when Khadija promised to leave. *What exactly is a marriage if there are no kids?*

And here is Yasmeen, her name a flower, Yasmeen of the spring.

He looks at his child in his arms and he thinks *you may be named for a flower but I do not think you will be a child of gardens and trees.*

His men were assembled, they had their arms at their backs.

I hear Khadija is expecting. May you be blessed with a son.

May you have a healthy child and never mind if it is a boy or a girl.

Have you and Khadija spoken of names?

We think Ahmed for a boy and Yasmeen if it is a girl.

Yasmeen? It is a pretty name but it is hardly the name for the leader of a revolution. Yasmeen? All I see are gardens and trees.

It is a delicate name. You know a child grows into their name.

I think of leaders and I cannot imagine following a woman named Yasmeen.

There is time yet and perhaps you will come to a name other than Yasmeen.

His men, his brothers in the cause, arrived one by one to congratulate him on his daughter's birth. If they were armed, their weapons were concealed. Each one bore a small bouquet. The bouquets were collections, varied in their flowers, but each one had yasmeen. They handed him their flowers and a small envelope with whatever sum they could afford. They asked to see her, passing her from hand to hand like a parcel, kissing her head and then her cheek.

Abdullah watched them whispering a prayer as they held her and he thought *she will have many uncles, those of blood and those who are tied to her by life.*

As they left, each in his own time, they stopped before him.

There is no name as fitting as hers.

There will come a day and she will be a leader and she will be followed by everyone.

We think our sons will be ours but it is a daughter that will look after her family and the future of the country.

I once dreamed that if I had a daughter her name shall be Yasmeen.

Once they were gone, he turned to Khadija and Yasmeen. The little one was asleep. Already it seemed that the only possibility was that her name should be Yasmeen.

INTO THE HILLS

Her father had promised her a surprise. 'You must not speak of this place I show you. It has been a secret for many years and our survival may depend on it staying secret.'

Yasmeen promised, she promised again, and he patted her arm and helped her into the car. Two hours they drove into the hills, then the mountains, till they were above the clouds. He stopped the car and told her to step out. 'Watch your feet. Follow my steps.'

Fog swirled at her ankles and the ground was visible only in patches. It made her fearful that she could not see what was beneath her feet.

THE DAY OF THE FLAGS

Her father shook her awake. 'Enough sleep. Let us go out and get some things.'

Yasmeen wanted to return to sleep but she remembered then what such outings meant. They would walk to the markets, they would breakfast on a table of her favourite foods, he would buy her sweets, they would go to the park with the well and the birds.

She could wake early for that.

She dressed quietly and she heard him moving around the house, she heard his whistle and she smiled. When he began to sing, she thought of her mother waking to tell him to keep his voice down before returning to sleep.

They walked together on the streets, the houses of their neighbours shuttered. There was none of the activity there would be later in the day. No rugs being dried, no floors being mopped, no families having their coffee out the front of the home. It was only them and he asked her about school and her friends and the families of her friends. He told her the latest political news, he told her about the meetings of yesterday, and how his brother had decided to pack up his kids and leave for the south. 'They do not see that this place will change in time. The things that others have in their lives we will have too. One day, the village school will be enough, and you and the children here will go there to learn. Those who are ill and unwell will be looked after in their old age and the brightest of our people will make their future here. Give it time. After decades of fighting, it will take a few years for the dust to settle but this land will know peace once more.'

She told him about her teachers, the planting of lemon and olive trees, of the books she read every night. He touched her hair, smoothing a loose strand, teasing her about the red ribbon tied at her crown. 'The money I have spent on ribbons, I could have built a bridge from here to the moon.'

'It isn't that much.'

'Maybe then from here to the south.'

His hand was on her shoulder as they waited for a clearing in the traffic so they could cross.

She studied the buildings around, the empty balconies, their sides unadorned.

'Dad?'

'Yes, Yasmeen?'

'There are no flags today.'

His hand on her shoulder drew her closer to his side. He frowned and then smiled and even at eight she knew he smiled for her. 'The flags will come out later in the day.' He was quiet, a lone post in a world of betrayals and plots. He stared around at the buildings and she knew he was searching for something on the balconies, a sign, a person, and she saw it before he did.

She squeezed his hand. 'There is a gun up there.'

He kept his head on the street ahead. He did not raise his eyes. 'Come, let us go home. Walk. Pretend you have seen nothing.'

That is what they did. They walked a hundred metres at a normal pace and the minute they were away from the buildings, he picked her up and ran.

HOSTILITIES

Abdullah returned from the meeting with Yasmeen.

What are these meetings? Meeting after meeting and what do they achieve?

Khadija was sitting in the darkness, not a single light on in the house. She had heard what had happened. To stay informed about the world, all you require is a telephone call. There had been a gunman, there had been some shots. In English, they say one sees red but she had seen black.

It was only a few shots before he was killed.

Only a few shots? Tell me: how many shots does it take for my daughter and husband to be killed?

They arrived just after nine. There she was in the dark. He turned on the light and saw her sitting there, still as a spider.

Why are you sitting in the dark?

Because I know not to make myself a target.

She tried to be calm but she spat out the words and he urged Yasmeen to go to her room.

It is not what you heard.

What is it then?

He was quickly taken care of.

A gunman shoots at you and it no longer registers. It is nothing notable, it is an event, one of many in a day.

It is not like that.

Then what is it? Tell me how I am wrong.

She had not meant to sweep her arm, she had not meant to overturn the photographs and the cabinet that held them. She had not meant to break so many of their precious things.

You are upset. We will speak in the morning.

He went to their room. She stayed where she was. For a week she slept in the living room, *let the neighbours think what they want.* They sat opposite each other at breakfast, lunch and dinner without exchanging a word. Only Yasmeen chattered, the sounds of a young child. They smiled at her, told her to eat her food, reminded her to read her books, to not waste all her time playing with her toys.

It was the end of the week, seven days not a single word between them, and they were seated for their dinner. Yasmeen broke the silence and spoke.

When are we going to a meeting again?

Khadija remembered then the children they had lost before they had Yasmeen. Four miscarriages, two dead soon after birth, and then Yasmeen, a miracle after they had given up all hope. She thought to entice her daughter away from Abdullah and his dreams, to shower her with games and puzzles and outings so she would forget these meetings of his. She thought to do it and she believed she could win, but there were enough battlegrounds outside and she would not have their daughter turned into one as well.

He was quiet and Yasmeen asked her question again.

He did not answer so she answered for him.

It will be next week. We will go together Thursday after school.

He said nothing, she said nothing, but later that day they suspended their hostilities and spoke once again.

THE POET SPEAKS

And then the poet, Nisrene:
   The just warrior
   for each part action
   allow two for reflection.
   Every day there is fighting
   follow with two in prayer.
   We may be fighters.
   Remember   our legacy   our children
   not weapons of war
   but gardens of learning and poetry.
   In the days of fighting,
   let there be no fear.
   Beyond the days of trouble,
   the world's false nod to peace,
   there is our single dream:
   our children in a garden,
   there they slumber, there they dream.
   The warrior knows the battle.
   The warrior's end   when peace begins.
   The garden is named for the daughter.
   Every flower shall be yasmeen.

PROPAGANDA

They mean to erase us from the face of the Earth.

This is one continuous tale of dispossession and displacement.

Once they have burned our books, once our language has been buried underground, once our culture is of the fiction past, then it will be too easy for them to say: did they even exist?

How do you strip people of their land? First you take their language and then you outlaw their beliefs. When they cry foul, you insist it is all in their heads.

Attach a rumour of barbaric acts to them. History will do the rest.

Say they are primitive, say they do not know this is for their own good.

Once injustice is dead, it will find life somewhere else.

Much of politics is fiction. It is the hall of smoke and mirrors. People look to their leaders for leadership, they look to them for the path. Trying to isolate the truth is like trying to find the needle in the haystack of lies.

You can sell people anything. It's a matter of how you sell it, the degree of spin.

The ultimate activity of a government is to justify itself. This is done by reciting statistics of achievement. If there aren't achievements to satisfy the masses, create a disturbance, draw their eyes next door. See! There is instability there. Would you rather this government or the one that rules next door?

Keep them distracted. Give them an enemy. This will keep their hatred occupied.

Each person wishes to sleep easy at night. One has to believe their self fair and kind and just. Equip them with the details so they can achieve their peace.

People! Watch the government that is always watching you.

THEIR WORDS

Her mother:

You think to shape the revolution but it will shape you more. The revolution has one owner and that is itself. The river is a force and to keep your head you stay out of its way.

Politics is a dirty game. Once you begin to play, it is impossible to keep your hands clean.

I told your father to leave so we could have a normal life. He could be a father and earn an honest wage but he cared for a country and a cause that cared zero for him.

I prayed every day for this madness to leave our lives.

You begin as an activist in the revolution and you believe the revolution's end is victory. Cure yourself of this delusion because there are few victories. Instead there is bloodshed and betrayal, and the death of millions becomes a note in history.

Stop and ask yourself: why do you do this and what do you hope to achieve? You can keep your intentions pure but the rest is beyond your control.

Your father's mistake was listening to people. He trusted them, giving them voice over his own judgement. To stay true is to ride a horse. You keep your eyes ahead and ignore the dogs on each side.

Her father:

The truth will prevail and my people will have their freedom if there is justice in this world.

I think always of my daughter and the world I wish for her. Shall I leave her a legacy of trouble and discord?

We will fight till none of us remain. Even after we are gone, we do not concede defeat.

The fighter knows that once he has fought, there will eventually be peace, and then the fighter will not recognise the world anymore.

I do this for you and the children you will have. I think of no one but my family and for us to have peace like the people of other nations.

Her words:

I did not mean for any of this. You wish for one thing and the world ends up giving you something entirely else. This is the way of the world but it is not easy when you pray for peace and end up with a war instead.

THE BULLY: PART I

In politics, there are always three figures. They are the bully, the sidekick and then the expendables.

Yasmeen, you need to determine quickly who the bully is. He is not hard to identify. Sometimes you will doubt he is the one. He smiles and says *come and be my friend* but ask yourself about everyone: what are their words and then what do they do?

This is the bully. He will show force. He will choose someone weak and make an example of them. That weak one is the expendable. It could be this person, it could be that. It does not matter to the bully. That expendable is a tool, a piece to be moved around as he pleases.

If you have trouble identifying the bully, consider their actions and the aftermath. Sometimes a person will resort to violence and there is no history of violence. There are apologies, there are tears. Chances are there are legitimate reasons. This person is not a bully. In the instance of the bully, there will be an action and there will be violence. Afterwards, people will feel the need to toe the line. They will look to the bully more and more for assurance. *Is it alright if I do this? Bully, do I have your permission?* This is the sidekick that speaks.

Beware the sidekick. Every bully has one. They are sheltered by the power of the bully. They pay however the sidekick is made to pay. The sidekick dreams himself free because he has this strong friend and perhaps this is true for now.

That is the bully, that is the sidekick.

And the third? That is everyone else. They are the expendables. They have a cause or they do not. They are visionaries or perhaps they are not. You see them in the street, you see them next door, and it is this group that will be swept aside as the bully makes his claims or the sidekick asserts his meagre strength.

You see here that there are three and none of them are free.

Do not forget that the bully is not found in politics alone. He can be the corporation, he can be the elected official, he can be the organisation that professes to do good, he can be the individual that is poisoning the river where the animals come to drink.

Find the bully. Study him and his friends. Keep your distance for now but remember he cannot be left too long unchecked.

THE ASSASSINS

In the name of Allah, the Most Compassionate, the Most Merciful.

Our adversary shall know defeat. This land is one way and he thinks to make it another. Already the plans are made so that the obstacle of his cause is dismantled piece by piece. His followers shall be removed in the manner they deserve.

Those who are true will keep their hearts clean.

When it is time to act, a single swipe and his undoing shall be done in one clean sweep.

THE ASSASSINATION

And it is an old story, her father said. *The day you were born, they turned up to the hospital one by one.* This is the story that ended with *these men are my brothers and if something happens to me you are to go to them.*

The story, no matter the retellings, ended the same each time.

What is the difference between death and assassination?

One is private and allows for grief. The other is a public killing of a figure and the world does not recognise there are family and friends.

Q: Why did the chicken cross the road?
A: To avoid being assassinated.

An assassination is not an isolated event. It is preceded by many attempts.

These men are my brothers, they are my friends.

Her father said to her once: a man is not betrayed by a stranger. A man is betrayed by a person who is known. Usually it is the one counted as brother and friend.

Those who aspire to political greatness must keep their ears alert, their eyes watchful. No news should be dismissed as unimportant. If you hear gossip and rumours, remember in the world they have their source.

She remembers statistics, she establishes the sequence of events. She strikes through her list, questioning her trust and if it is justified.

There is one name that is whispered and she knows it can only be him.

She sends out word. *He is to be brought to me. He is to be brought to me alive.*

She imagines the day, she imagines her words. They are to have weight, they are to be great.

Instead she faces him and she thinks *he trusted you with his life.*

She meant to stay, she meant to see it done, but she leaves. She does not need to see this.

Her father's words: we are in the business of politics. There will be betrayal but never forget your humanity.

THE RAT

To be a rat is to make your plots and to leave room for an escape.

To be a rat is to be a leader who makes a historic deal. You sign your name and the people will butcher each other in the streets. Short term they call it betrayal. Long term they will only remember peace.

To be a rat is to remember the future is an arc. It was heading to the left but now it will instead turn to the right.

To be a rat is to forget the person and to focus your mind on the political. The political is not personal. The other version is a lie.

To be a rat is to accept that the popular view and yours do not align. Do not trouble over this. Each must march to the beat of his own drum.

To be a rat is to search for an opportunity. See the sky through the clouds. This is your chance.

To be a rat is to don a role. You will sell out the saviour, you will orchestrate the fall of the Moor. You will be asked to betray him, the one you count as a brother and a friend. His daughter calls you Uncle. You must realise that what is demanded of you is greater than one person or two. Today they will not understand but, in the writing of history, you will find your peace.

AN ODE TO REASON

Miss, they have blown up the ruins. I went there and saw it with my own eyes. Miss, I thought you said they wouldn't touch the ruins. My family were sheltering there. I looked for them but there are no bodies, only rubble. I only pray that they are not buried beneath. Miss, tell me, what remains of us once they have destroyed our history, once they have killed our people, once our existence has been wiped from the Earth? They will place no markers for our dead. My mother was put in a grave with a hundred others and till now I do not know where she rests. I have no one left, just you and this cause. I gave you my children, I gave you my brothers and sisters, and we all fought for this thing we believe in but I fear now there will be nothing left. I am a small man and they are so much bigger than us. What does it matter to them or to anyone whether I live or die? I am not afraid to die, none of us are afraid to die, and you know I do not speak out of fear, but I fear them now, I fear the enemy where the living are nothing in his regard, where the fighter and the civilian are targets alike, who goes to war, not for a cause he believes in but for the love of fighting, to show the world his weapons, to tell the world he is a man and he is to be feared. I am afraid, miss. I thought we each fought for our reasons, but I hear them say it now. His reasons live out in a land beyond life, and he has no respect, no honour, he is one indifferent to the world, and I fear now you have been reasoning with the one who will not respond to reason.

Forgive me, my lady, but today I am afraid.

ABU BAKR

They capture him at dawn. His scalp is a big prize, their biggest prize yet. He reminds her of her grandfather. He is dressed in the same loose pants, he has sandals on his feet and socks on for it is winter. Watching him, you would be fooled into thinking him a harmless old man.

Her people bring her the news. 'It is him. It is Abu Bakr.'

They have bound his wrists and his ankles. His mouth is free for now.

She has dreamed of this day. He is one step on the road to victory.

'Speak. What trouble brings you here?'

He spits at her feet. 'I will not speak to a whore.'

Her grandfather, already in the next life, would never have spoken such a word. One of her fighters lunges at Abu Bakr, sticking a knife to his throat. 'The traitor thinks to speak of honour. Silence now or it will be your tongue.'

She urges them to bring Abu Bakr to his feet. She stares into his eyes. It is years that they have fought, once alongside each other, but she will not show mercy to a traitor. His treachery cost her a thousand on the first day. Since then, they have been cut off, her people are starving in the hills, the world watches blackly on.

'You sold us. Was it for money?'

'You are a child. You do not belong in the wars of men. Go to your dresses and your pretty things. A woman does not belong in the battle but in the home. You thought to fight for a dream but the dream is dead. He taught you to believe and you cling to his words even though they are foolishness. This is their war, it will have no end. It is better to make a deal for your people. Perhaps they will even let you live. You cannot blame me. I have a family. I have daughters and they are like you. I do not ask for your mercy. I know you will kill me but show reason. This war cannot be won.'

She gives the signal. They raise their swords. 'This war is done when it has been won.'

One clean sweep and his head is free. She will leave him—a reminder—to those who shelter in the dark.

THE PHOTOGRAPH

Yasmeen remembers the photograph. She remembers his rage. She remembers her father waking her in the night crying, 'This will turn the world against us.' She had woken in the morning and thought it was a dream except there was the paper and there was the face—unmistakable—of the man he had trusted with his life. A minute later the embassy blew up. 'How do you think this will make us look? This will be in the face of the world. It does not matter how we explain this. The words we say will matter for nothing.' He sat back and held his head in his hands. She did not hear him at first but there was his whisper. 'The world is against us.'

Her mother hit his arm. 'Do not judge now. Judge when this is over.'

'It does not matter,' he said. 'It does not matter.'

He had been right. The world turned against them. Yesterday they were the flavour of the month. Now they are outside on the fringe. A month or two, and their supporters, their suppliers disappeared. The directive was to quietly shut things down and he would have done it if he could, but the world fought over his name and what he meant and what he stood for without him saying a word.

He said this. He meant this. His man was there. He is not our ally. He is an enemy to be hunted down.

When he was killed, she went through her days in a fog but she could not say she was surprised. His life was summed up, timelined, this was now the official version. She banned news in the compound.

It is over, it does not matter, the world is no longer on our side.

Her people turned up for his burial. The world pretended he was not a man, he had no family. There was no one to remember his name and what he really said, what he truly believed.

It does not matter.

She hated the world. She woke in a rage, she went to bed furious. They turned him into a monster. The path he had followed was twisted into a misshapen thing.

He has died. Let this cause die with him.

She would have left it but they called for her. She ignored them. 'I have my child, I have this life.' They continued to call. She would have continued to ignore them except for her dream. He held the photograph and he pushed it in her face. 'This is not the truth. You shall make the world see what is true and what is not.'

She did not believe as he had believed. She did not have the fire as he did in her heart but when they asked for her in the morning, she bowed her head and said, 'I will do what must be done.'

She said this and she was afraid.

It is over.

It does not matter.

The world is no longer on our side.

She agreed and it was then she saw her end.

THE PLUMS OF SPRING

For Peter Skrzynecki

Yasmeen, there is the dream and then there is wakefulness, and in the first few moments of waking, it is difficult to distinguish between the two.

She has been dreaming. Lately all she does is dream. Her mother reminds her sleep is for rest but one who takes to their bed in the day is troubled by something else. *Won't you speak to your mother and tell me what it is that bothers you?*

Her mother is in the dream. Her father speaks from a height on the Day of Troubles to their people below. 'We will not be driven from this land. We will not hide in the mountains like thieves. With God as my witness, I say to the world that my people shall be free.'

My people shall be free. He says this to her after the crowds have gone their way, after they are alone once more. 'I see now that before me I have my destiny and that to fight it is pointless. I have been put on this Earth for one reason and that is so that we will be free.'

She cries. Freedom, a long-held dream, will finally be theirs. He does not see—neither does she—what her mother has always warned. 'You think to lead them to victory but the world will make a martyr of you.'

She cries then and there are tears many other times and on the day he is shot publicly and paraded like a trophy in the emptiness of the streets.

My people shall be free.

The world will make a martyr of you.

They both ignore the warnings, they do not read the signs as they have been read by others.

The world has turned on you.

The weather is not favourable to your cause.

The warning is offered and the warning is ignored.

She will have her turn too. *My daughter, it is time to leave, it is time for us to leave, do you mean to be turned into a toy for those more powerful than you?*

She takes to her bed and she begins to dream. He is her father, no more. They walk in the garden and it is spring. The trees are in blossom. Soon they will be heavy, the plums bloody with the colour of life. They walk and the garden is silent except for the birds and the breeze. *The world is most beautiful in spring. Did you know you were a child born in spring and these trees remind me of that time you were born?*

My people shall be free.

Leave that to the plots and turns of the world.

The trees remind me of that time you were born.

She takes to her bed and she hears his whisper. The tree is heavy with plums, the garden is in a state of neglect and it is spring but soon enough it will be winter, and if spring is for birth, then winter is when the innocent will lose their lives.

THE MOTHER OF THE WORLD

Yasmeen dismisses her general and sits with her son. He asks her questions, one fired after the other as she once did to her father. He does not give her time to answer before he asks the next. She tickles him to make him stop but Bilal laughs and slaps her away.

A few minutes more and then she must leave. There is her son but then there is also the revolution and her people. She walks through the compound, the concrete smooth beneath her feet. She stands in her room and checks no one is hiding in the shadows for her like that time. If her son had been with her, she would have killed them with her bare hands, but not this time. There are flowers, the window is open. She smells yasmeen, in bloom this time of year, and remembers her mother.

This will not be a good life for you. Leave this. Someone else will lead them. Your duty is to yourself, your son and to God. It is to no one else. This is a dirty business. The wicked prosper and the innocent pay with their lives. You know this. I have told you this before. We can leave. There is time yet to leave. Come, leave this all behind.

She does not leave. She stays. Her general is new, the last one paid with his life.

The wicked prosper and the innocent pay with their lives.

She wants revenge for his death but she has lost track. So much justice owed and she forgets for what and to whom.

She washes quickly and then she prays. She says her thank you to God, that she has been given this day, that it counts as mercy if she is given one more.

Bilal comes to her and climbs in at her side. She holds him to her, already drifting away. He started doing this when General M was blown away. Bilal says nothing and it does not take him long to fall asleep.

She thinks of her son and her people who come to her for protection. Once, her father stood between her and the world, but since his passing there is no one. It is her alone, standing as a shield between her people and the world.

BROKER THE PEACE

'Your people are rioting in the streets. Do you realise the damage they have caused?'

She counts: three dead, four hundred and twenty-two injured, six thousand police officers deployed, another five thousand on stand-by, three military units, the riot squad brought in from the capital.

And the damage they have caused: four burnt buses, one hundred and nine shops looted, ten police cars overturned, the public fountain, the statue of the incumbent leader destroyed.

Thirty thousand on the streets, the millions watchful at home.

'Do you realise the damage they have caused?'

She thinks: political prisoners, fugitives, hundreds detained, those lost to fighting, those classified in absentia or at large.

She thinks: migration, expulsion, exile, ending unknown.

She thinks: do you realise the damage you have caused?

It is her father. It was an early lesson. There is the saying he said. 'It is better to die on your feet than live on your knees.' Then there is the novel he read. 'The narrator is quick to dispense death because he has not yet learned to live. So, you see, there is a lesson here. A mind engaged with its world must be able to occupy contradictory truths. Yes, it is better to live on one's feet but do not idolise death over life. That shows a poverty of spirit. Such is the tendency of one who has not yet learned to live.'

'You say you wish for peace but you advocate resistance for your cause. Your methods are fighting and violence. Your people are no better than the barbarians of old. You think your band of fighters—no more than murderers and thieves—will teach us a lesson of defeat, but history will be written by the mighty and one day your name will be synonymous with defeat.'

She thinks: my people are sovereign. We will not be denied our freedom and peace.

He showed her the hills. 'Our people have sheltered here throughout the years. Once the cities have failed you, there is still the refuge of the hills.'

'Where do you think this will end? These riots, this chaos, what face does it show to the world? We are for a truce. It will be symbolic, a handshake, no more.'

She thinks then of her father. She thinks of his stories about the resistance and its start. She thinks of telling him about the single-mindedness of a cause and how he laughed and laughed till he began to cry. Were they tears of laughter or did her father weep?

'The resistance has many paths. You think them clear but they are vague at best. A few end in victory but most end in defeat.

You weigh the price of your choices and you act in the way you think best but you are not alone. For your action, the world will respond with a thousand of its own. You make your choice but ultimately it is the world that will write the story's end.'

TWENTY-EIGHT

They take their coffee on the balcony, the city cast in morning light. The flag—red and white—hangs from windows, it stands on the rooftops they can see. Once upon a time they played a game. Saleh counted the red and white, she counted the symbols of the cause. The numbers went his way and some other days they went hers, but often they met halfway and it would be the basis of a joke.

Today they ignore the flag and their conversation takes a different course. There is his work at the university, there is Bilal's progress in school, there is the celebrity who brings her people here to holiday by the beach.

She comments on the teacups, he comments on the necklace she wears.

It was a gift from her father from when she was eight. It is two circles intertwined, a symbol worn on both sides of the divide. She realises she has never worn it with him before, that she has always favoured jewellery that makes her affiliations clear. Since his death, she has abandoned her other jewellery for simple pieces and nothing else.

'Why do you give her this necklace that means nothing? These circles are so common, they are cheap,' her mother said.

'Perhaps one day she will have the need for common things.'

She wears this necklace now and she thinks of her father and how his face once was in so many windows, their flag on the rooftops, how their cause lived upon the streets. Now there is no need to count and there is red and white as far as the eye can see. The obviousness of this lies unsaid between them and she wonders about the faces borne by defeat.

All this red and white and her father gone from the world and Saleh is silent except for words about the jewellery she wears. She searches the buildings, searching for a sign, when he says, 'Your father is over there.'

It is her father's face, the photograph taken when he was twenty-eight. He is so young, his face not yet worn by the world. He once said to her, 'I was most hopeful when I was twenty-eight. The hope I knew then belongs to another age and I will never feel that hope again.'

His face is lost between the flags and she wonders about this turn of events. She wears a common necklace and Saleh counts the photos for her father's side.

'He is so young.'

And he has not yet been destroyed by the world and it is a different age, but between those red and white flags, there is his picture and forever he will be twenty-eight.

THE VERSION OF EVENTS

Saleh watches the boy who blinks in the sun. He is young, seven perhaps, and his face is much like hers. He knows the boy's name but he does not use it because Bilal is not known to him.

Bilal talks to the other kids, he carries a bag with a picture of a motorcycle on his back, he moves the hair out of his face.

Bilal leaves the gates and walks towards his home. He says hello to neighbours, he calls out to his friends. He does not see the stranger that follows him, studying him for signs of someone else.

He closes in on him and calls out Bilal's name.

The boy turns towards him, his face free of fear, full of trust for his world. Bilal stares up at him. 'My mother had a photo of you. I saw it once in her room.'

He wonders what he meant to say to this boy when Bilal is at best a connection to someone else.

'Come. I will buy you ice cream and then I will take you home.'

They walk together and he slows his pace to match the boy's. Bilal talks about the town, the streets and the houses, he talks about the people who live in this place. He eats his ice cream and then they walk to his home. A street before, he says goodbye and lets him walk to the house alone.

He wonders what the neighbours will make of this stranger, what Bilal will say about his day, but he does not care because in the boy's face is the memory of hers.

It is their ritual. Thursday after school they go for ice cream and then Bilal walks to his home. He is surprised when Khadija walks in, introduces herself and addresses him as Saleh. He assumes Yasmeen kept him separate from the rest of her world and he does not expect Khadija to know the details of his life, let alone his name. They speak about the weather and the events of the day and then she sends Bilal to order for her.

'In a month we leave for the south and then perhaps we will go abroad. There is no future for us here anymore.'

He thinks of the cause, he thinks of the flags, he thinks of Yasmeen's father and then finally of her. He does not say a word.

'I opposed this from the start. We fought so much over the years and it was all hidden because he was the face of his cause, and I would say to myself it is okay, it is alright, these days will pass, there is hope, but now I see something else. Perhaps if I had fought more, I would still have him and I would still have her. Do you know it took me ten years to have her and I had almost given up, and now she is gone and all I have is that boy? These thoughts keep me up at night and I think, what if she had not hidden you? What if she had shown you to the world? Together you both would have been the symbol of something else and she would not have died so soon. They thought to stand for an idea and there are so many who prize an idea over a life. They have paid with their lives but this boy will have his life. He did not know his father, he does not have a mother, but he will have a normal life. Perhaps one day the world will listen and their cause will come good but I will not have him turned into someone's toy.' She smiles then and he thinks of how much she resembles Yasmeen. 'But this is silliness and I talk of foolish things. I opposed them and their cause, but it seems the world turns us all into fighters and for some a child can be a cause.'

He wants to argue with her, he wants her to say her daughter's name, but Bilal returns and she finishes her ice cream quickly and then they leave.

Later, he could have continued to see Bilal, perhaps he could have visited them at their house, but he left it. When he reads in the paper that they have moved away, there is a photograph of Yasmeen with her father. There are the mountains, there is their flag, there are the words attributed to them. He studies her father's face first and then finally he looks at hers.

She is young and this is before they ever met.

Her face is that of a figure, at once familiar and removed. He thinks the world will settle on a version, her life will be written again and again, but there will be no disputing her world has come to an end.

THE TRUTH IN WORDS

Lately Bilal is troubled by dreams, lately he wonders what he knows to be real.

For example: in class, he learns about his grandfather and mother and he is grateful for his common family name. These are the details of their lives. This was her life, this was his. They debate his grandmother who has taken to tending the garden more and more. She has her fruit trees and there is yasmeen and she has let the vines form a green wall. She says it is to offer them privacy but he suspects she means to wall them in and he leaves her. She is an old woman. Let her have her comforting things.

His teacher continues to talk in his dream, but in the distance Yasmeen and Abdullah run. The world is a roar and it is in his ears but they are getting away.

He chases after them but they are too quick for him and just once he wants her to look back and acknowledge him.

These dreams wake him and send him walking through their home while the rest of the world is asleep. He walks to the kitchen and fills his cup and he sees the door is open that leads outside.

Khadija is seated before her trees, she tells him she loves the night more and more, that this is the only time in the day she is at peace.

Bilal remembers then a night many years ago when he asked her to speak of their lives and the people they had been. She dismissed him—this disturbance of a child—and he went away in tears. He thinks of that night as she pats the bench near her.

Sometimes it is easy to forget the stories he has heard and to see this woman before him.

She points to the flowers. 'We named her after a flower because flowers are pretty things. We name her for a flower, we name her for a bird or a tree. In the end, does it matter? These are just words. These are sounds to fill the silence between human beings.'

He has heard people are naming their boys Abdullah and their girls Yasmeen, and even Khadija is popular again.

'Some days I think he was my husband and he was known to me. I read his words every day, private words he wrote to me, and I try to find him but he no longer belongs to me. The public and the private cannot be told apart because he now belongs to history. So I come here, I sit with my trees, and I have names for every single tree, and I know his name and I know hers but I have abandoned my search. They lived, they died, and I knew them in that time, but they will be never known to me.'

He thinks then of the stories, the morals attached to this woman who looks after him. They say she is to blame, they say she could have stopped the cause with a word. They say the three are equally to blame and she deserves her share of a third.

He thinks of all this but these are words and the truth lies somewhere else. Bilal settles into this sentence as he returns to his bed. He believes these words are his but they belong to someone else. They are a turn on a line his grandfather once said.

'Politics is all words. Remember, the truth is somewhere else.'

In the name of Allah, the Most Compassionate, the Most Merciful.

Each person has their fate, each person has their turn.

There are the people who will meet their end at the bottom of this well. It keeps their secrets, it keeps their tears when they weep.

I listen for I can do no else. It is the destiny of a creature of my kind to be condemned, to be trapped by a forlorn place.

I am used to this. It has been a long life. I cherish the dream of freedom still. Circumstances may permit me one more liberated turn.

This is not my story. These are their stories, ones I have been offered, others accidentally heard.

To be trapped is to be turned into a listener, to come by the knowledge that the story of life has no beginning, no end and is as old as the Earth.

Um Kareem came here with tears in her eyes after the town had gone to sleep. It was not the first time. I counted four previous visits, those for which I'd been awake.

She came with her eyes red and left with her face redder still. Often she went to sleep with a headache.

Her trouble was simple. Abu Kareem wanted to marry again and it did not matter what tricks, what prayers she used, she could not get him to return to their bed.

He could marry again. It was his right, she—Um Kareem—would not stand in his way, but he wished for her and his new wife to live together under the same roof, a situation that could turn violent if Abu Kareem was not at home to keep the peace. Never mind it was Abu Kareem who was the source of her troubles. He was the reason she came to this isolated place in tears.

Their children were asleep. Everyone said they were good kids. They prayed every day, their hands were always busy around the house. *They are innocent, they are curious, they have a special sense of the world.*

Lately she notices them not talking to their father. They do not greet him when he first walks in. They use the excuse of their homework. Their heads are down, *we did not see you come in.*

She notices when they put out the dinner, they now serve her first, which they never used to do, Abu Kareem commenting on the little they put on his plate.

They are polite children but they nudge the plate towards him and tell him to serve himself.

His clothes smell lately and he does not present as nicely to the world.

She notices they wash everything in the house—sheets, towels, socks—but they leave his clothes for last and they hang them in the shade. It takes them so long to dry this way and when she mentions this, they act innocent and say they ran out of space.

They are her three children, they are hers more than his. If she walked into fire, they would follow her, but to him they would turn their backs.

She kisses them once they are in bed. She checks their books to make sure their homework is done. They used to go out to play but now the three of them sit close together and watch cartoons on the TV.

Their dad says cartoons are from the devil, that too much TV will rot their brains.

And she cannot be sure but she thought the youngest had said *but cheating on your wife is halal*.

They could not know. It must be how her ears heard what they said, but she thinks of facing people, of acting normal, like she has not been dismissed, that there is not this new one, a better one, prettier perhaps, to take her place.

She thinks of her children—their children—at school having to hear the meanness that their classmates might say. She thinks of the teachers, the pity of people, how she will hold her head between people, how she will explain this so that there is no gossip behind their backs.

If she could take her children and live in a tent here, she would do it, but it would not be good for their learning, they would pay even more for the disagreements of their parents.

She has come to the well three times this week. It is a quiet place and she wishes she was a person who believed in making wishes that a creature then grants, but she makes no such wishes. She offers her tears and she leaves when she is dry. As she walks home, there is no one to comment on how she looks or how useless it is to cry.

Her son is dead. She does not know it yet. They will tell her in three weeks, but for now Amira has hope. Amira comes to the well because it is where she can remember Khaled so young, and this is the place he came to play with his friends. They climbed the trees till it was dark and one time they found a football to kick around. Khaled never told her where they got the football. She overheard his friends saying it was on the beach after a big storm but she believes they had stolen it from somewhere.

She remembers Khaled coming home with four of his friends, asking for a bucket because he had kicked the ball into the well. She emptied the potatoes onto the floor and gave him the bucket, telling him there was a rope behind the feed for the cow, that he needs to bring both back or else his father would kill him if they were not returned to their place.

They returned in an hour with the bucket, rope and ball, talking non-stop about their efforts to retrieve it, how they were ready to abandon the project when Ahmed suggested one more go.

They laughed and passed the ball around, and *yes, yes, we'll return the potatoes to the bucket and the rope to its original place.*

They continued to meet at the well and Amira is certain this is where Khaled and his friends first learned to smoke. She can still remember her husband's rage when Khaled lit a cigarette after dinner, casually, as if it was his habit all along. Farooq threatened to fill Khaled's mouth with chilli if he dared smoke before his parents again.

Khaled put out his cigarette, he apologised and avoided looking at his father's face, but the truth was out and a week later he lit another cigarette and this time Farooq did not make a sound.

She imagines them as young men sharing a cigarette, sneaking the tobacco when their parents were looking the other way.

Yesterday Farooq found her in the orchard and he touched her arm.

'There were so many times I wanted to kill him when he was younger. He could be a devil, especially when he was with his friends. There has been silence this last week and I ask every day for God to protect him from the same end as his friends.'

She told him Khaled could not send word and that was the reason for his silence and that always she kept her hope.

She considers her hope now and how this place is heavy with a presence, how the children joke that these abandoned places are where the dead are buried, right under people's noses where their bones will not be troubled by the feet of the living overhead.

There *is* a presence here. She feels it close to the well. It is the presence of the living and she speaks to it, ignoring the stories of how demons are drawn to water, because that is not the sense that she gets. Whatever lives here, she speaks to, and all her life she has felt it to be a friend.

Idris was now fifteen but he had the mind of a two year old. She still dressed him, she bathed him, she fed him because if anyone saw him eat, they would think him no better than a beast.

In the night, she let him loose, and the next day she heard stories of where he had wandered to. Their village was quiet in the night-time and the few cars slowed because of bumps in the surface of the road and because no one wanted to hit their neighbour's cat or cow.

If they could take care to avoid the animals, they could do the same for her boy.

It had been a difficult day and none of her efforts had managed to calm Idris. She found him on the roof in the afternoon when he should have been sleeping, and he refused to give her the rocks he had been throwing at the cars. She twisted his hands and took them from him as she pinned him to the ground.

He cried, of course he cried, and when he cried, he was loud and he could be heard in the houses around. Um Kareem stopped by with the eggs and she tickled Idris until laughter replaced his cries.

That boy needs a school. He is too much for you, and she knew this, she had heard these words all the days of Idris, and with the situation, it was not safe for them to leave the village, but the truth was she did not believe Idris could be helped by any school. Yes, they could put him in a nappy like a baby, they could feed him with a spoon as she did, they could leave him free to walk between brick walls, but at least here, their neighbours knew to look after him. She went to the supermarket once a week and sometimes Idris walked in by himself. He'd have oranges and berries or whatever was growing in their neighbours' trees.

She knew about the school, of course she did. She prayed for him as the religious had recommended in the past. Hadn't she been with them when they read from the Book over his head and asked the demons to leave his body so he could live like the free? There had been many of these sessions and at them Idris often fell asleep.

She did not worry about the effect of these sessions. When Idris woke, she checked his eyes and knew him unchanged, and she remembered the line about the crooked rib. His life had its own shape and to straighten it would break it and Idris was best left alone.

He walked the streets as his mother did. She came here after midnight because she would not see anyone. In the day, there was a crowd of children, the men played their chess, the women brought their coffee here to enjoy in the sun.

There had been talk of putting in lights for the night-time but the village had bigger troubles, as did the country, and a few lights could wait.

People were fighting their neighbours, people carried guns in the cities when they went out in the streets. She heard the advice about locking doors and windows, staying inside because *let us not forget there is a war going on*.

Some days, she wondered about solutions. Some days, she wondered about Idris and his end and she thought about taking him like a stray animal and releasing him a great distance from their house.

She would be free of him then.

She would be free and she trusted the world to look after him because God looked after the simple better than the smart, and did Idris even know she was his mother, and wouldn't he be served by a stranger just as well?

She had thought this before, she had thought it many times, but there was a voice this time and it spoke from the bottom of the well.

'He has been given to you. His life is not for you to decide. Leave this foolishness and cleanse your heart with prayers before going to bed.'

There had been stories about this place, of people having visions, but she had never believed. She would have fled but her feet were stuck and she heard the words in her heart.

I have been foolish.

This is my destiny.

There is a God above.

She went home and checked on Idris. He was already in his bed. She kissed his forehead and touched his hair. For everyone there was a watcher but at least for the simple, no matter the situation in the world, it was better to believe that to them the universe was always kind.

Bilal had a name. Zein—or Zeineddine—once a revolutionary, Zein was now a mechanic. He had snuck out the small box of his mother's things when Khadooj was out, and he sat reading the letters carefully. He already knew about the other man, Saleh in the photograph, who now took him out for ice cream, and most of the other people referenced in the letters he already knew. They were part of his family's circle but this man Zein—or Zeineddine—was never mentioned, and Bilal was a smart cookie, and he believed that the search ended with him.

His grandmother gave him money to buy sweets after school, but Bilal brought all his money with him, and he asked his friends about the cost of a bus to the north. Together they pooled their information and he made a list of the bus stops and worked out how he'd know he had arrived in the village. Mustapha was smarter than he seemed and he told Bilal, 'You can ask the driver to tell you when you're in the village.'

Bilal bought apples and an orange to eat but he had no knife. He took the orange out and a soldier next to him peeled it with an old knife and smiled when Bilal gave him half. He looked out the window and none of these places were familiar to him. His grandmother had talked about doing trips north but mainly they went south and these days they stayed home more and more. Omar's family said they would go to the snow in the winter but Khadooj was already packing their things and Bilal believed that by the winter they would be living overseas, so better now to do this trip.

He asked in the shops, the butcher's, the bread place, he asked in the place selling women's clothes. Every instruction directed him closer until he stopped before the shop where Zein worked.

The man that approached him wiped his hands on his trousers and Bilal tried to imagine how his mother had met him. The country was small but this village was far and his mother had never had a car.

Zein stared at the boy who was smaller than he had imagined and he would have recognised him in any crowd because there was no mistaking Yasmeen's eyes.

He had expected this day but he had not expected the boy to come here by himself.

Zein told the others he was going for lunch and he would not return for a while. He told the boy to come with him, he asked after his name. It was Bilal, and he smiled at this, that Yasmeen had settled on the name he had suggested. He remembered they had argued this point, back when they argued, back when he was part of her life still.

She had startled him with the news and it upset him that life went on with its births and deaths, that this cycle answered to no one and nothing: not a revolution, not a war, not even the divisions that persisted even after her death, more than when she had been alive.

He did not want to go to the past like this, not when he was faced with his child.

Their lunch was two rolls and a soft drink that they shared in plastic cups. He asked Bilal if he wanted ice cream or something sweet and the boy said that was for later.

Bilal—it suited him—was either eight or nine. What could he say to this child who was so young, so foreign to him, a little mountain beyond his reach, much like Yasmeen had been?

He talked to Bilal about his village, he talked about this park, the well that had been empty his entire life. He made up stories to entertain Bilal and the scary ones left him unimpressed, but then this boy had seen so much in his life. Zein said there was a genie or a demon in the well, no one could say for sure, and when Bilal dismissed his stories, he said words that Bilal would remember as his father's words for the rest of his life.

'The world is ruled by the unseen as much as the seen, and the Creator controls the smallest details, even the things no man shall ever know.'

Bilal remembered this and the name Zeineddine and when people spoke of his father, he said, 'My father is not someone unknown to me . . .'

Yet Zein was not his father, not the presence a boy needed as he was growing up. His grandmother was more a father, his grandfather, there was that man his mother had known at the end of her life. He carried the memory of his father—the name and his few stories—along with the other fathers that life also provides. There is a cause, there is a land, he turns to his memories in the middle of the night. Khadooj did this too—a woman given to the past, who has shadows for company more and more. A name and a few words, and then there is his father, once a revolutionary and now just a small man in a forgotten park.

He needed the money. There was little left in his mother's pouch. Even if there had been money, he did not think money in this time could actually buy much.

When Sami asked him if he wanted to drive a truck from A to B and this is how much you'll be paid, Rashid knew there would be more than potatoes, no matter how many times Sami swore there were potatoes and nothing else.

The timing had to be exact. He had to reach the first checkpoint ten minutes after midnight. Bashir would be standing out the front. He was to make a comment about the mountains of the north, and with this, the truck would pass without being checked.

It was a point Sami stressed again and again.

You must be there at that time. It must be Bashir or they'll check the truck from top to bottom, and who knows with the army these days! They wouldn't mind the extra potatoes. The country is such a mess and nothing's getting in and my cousin tells me that by the wintertime if this situation doesn't change, the villages are going to starve. Who knows what they'll do in the cities with the fighting and no room to grow even a bit of grass?

Sami was right and the stories were worrying but Rashid still did not believe this business about the potatoes in the back.

The night started smoothly.

There is Bashir, his M16 on his back, chewing gum and cleaning his nails with a sharp stick in the checkpoint's poor light.

The mountains of the north are better than the ones in the south.

Bashir nods, asks what he has in the truck and takes a torch to look at the cascade of potatoes in the back. Satisfied, he nods, points out the road ahead, and wishes Rashid a safe trip to where the potatoes will come to rest.

Rashid cannot get the potatoes out of his mind and he stops in his village at the park. It is the only place he thinks he will be alone at this time of night. He takes his father's torch and shuts the truck's doors and moves the stack of potatoes from one side of the bed to the other, every single potato, and he finds there is nothing hidden underneath.

He feels like an idiot for wasting hours in a deserted park in the middle of the night, checking the potatoes one by one.

And he can't leave the potatoes like this otherwise they'll know he went through them, that he did not trust the story he had been fed.

So another hour and the potatoes are returned to their original formation, and he wonders about the early morning and how madness gets into a person's head.

He was certain there would be more than potatoes. Surely he's not going to be paid so well for some vegetables moved from place to place.

He doesn't believe it. It makes absolutely no sense. He was certain. He would have put money on it, he would have sworn on his mother's life.

There is more to these potatoes than meets the eye.

When he hears the voice, Rashid locks the door of the driver's seat and pretends he did not just hear the well speaking to him in the dark.

He knows about this park and he is sure one day he'll mark this as the day he lost his mind. Never mind, never mind. The potatoes to their destination and then he can get into his bed, and with his money he can plan the feast they'll have in the morning time.

There are many bodies buried in this ground.

Some of the dead are only bones.

Others are more recent. Their burial was hurried, done in the dark, ground covered so it did not appear disturbed.

I have watched for many years.

When the world is troubled, there are more secrets to put to sleep in the earth, in the night-time when they believe no eyes can see.

I watch. There are others—humans—who believe this park can shelter their terror and their dreams.

There is always the watcher, one of lightness on the right, the scribe of darkness on the left, and then the Great One who not even the smallest detail escapes.

The world may not see. There may be no witness in the living but the record is always kept. The weight of history is layers, and it does not disappear, no matter how oblivious is humanity.

Here comes the religious man, here he comes with his beard. He is like the new beard wearers who believe a beard can hide the dark way they choose to live.

I see him. Through the day, he goes to his religion. These days, there are so many like him. It never used to be like this.

He comes to the park. He sits at that bench. Before the eyes of the world, he brings her, the one they've learned to ignore.

When they see them together, they look elsewhere. Their gaze goes above their heads. Any lower and their eyes would meet and they would be faced with the lie they keep.

He has children. She has children. Her husband took them away overseas. She has not heard from them since. If her body was not marked, if her belly did not show it once was stretched, it would be easy to believe there was no husband or that they had four kids.

So she takes the bearded man to her bed. Hers is the only one in the town where they will have privacy. She does not mean to love him, he does not mean to love her. It started innocently. The wall of the fence had collapsed. He came around to help. A poor woman, brought to live here when she was married, and now she is alone in that house, not a sound from that husband wherever he is.

Remember! He only came to help. Now they sit together daily at that bench. His own wife tears at her hair and no one says it but her husband doesn't care.

They talk about returning to a friendship. This is a relationship no one will ever forgive. She should return to the town where her family live. What does she have here but that little house her husband left her?

She has friends, friends who are kind like him.

Lately, he goes to pray more and more. He leaves his work early, which he never used to do, to pray in the middle of the day. He stops to pray before he returns to his home and everyone notes the size of his beard.

He has a plan, he has spoken to the people he knows overseas. Many countries are taking migrants. If she wishes to leave, now is her chance. He has money he has hidden. *It is better for you to leave than be condemned to this lonely life between these village people here.*

She hears him. She believes him. She trusts him as she never trusted the one who disappeared.

She has no future, even less so than the other people she knows in this country. They speak of freedom, there are the movies of how else people can live. It is easy for her to believe in a better life, to believe it exists as more than a fantasy.

He promises her the money, he tells her about the plane that will take her away, he says he will rent out this place and send the small amount it will make to her.

Don't you believe it will be better because there is nothing for you here?

He is right. He is completely right. From here I can hear her crying over the difficulties of her life.

It is the last time they meet in this park. That night, he gives her the money, the ticket, he tells her about the passport and what has been organised. *Your flight is in a month and there is no reason for you to rely on a burdened man like me.*

They shake hands much like friends. She says goodbye to him for the final time. The next day, the people are glad. Their bench is empty and they can stare around the park without having to overlook what their eyes plainly see.

The lovers sneak here for privacy.

They are innocent still. They have not yet crossed an invisible boundary.

She holds his hand, he kisses her cheek.

Thunder, rain, the cold, the heat, nothing frightens them away. Even when there's a voice in the dark, they laugh because it is evidence of magic much like their love.

They make their plans.

There is an explosion in the sky.

Ash rains down and she holds out her hand at this black snow.

This is the darkness I wish to protect you from.

They have not told their parents. Soon they will, soon they will be public with their love.

It is easy to imagine the future. They will have a simple wedding, they will have children, they will live their lives in a few small rooms.

They will plant fruit trees. They will keep a garden. They will clean this park that harbours them, that allows them this privacy.

We can even clean out the well. I wonder if there is water in it still.

They say there is water but it is no good to drink.

They walk over, smiling at the voice that comes from the trees, the well that vibrates at their feet.

She looks down into the well.

He is aware of how close she is.

He does not tell her but she has a scent. It is flowers and it reminds him of spring. One day she will be known to him but now she is the world's greatest mystery.

It is night-time. The darkness is around them.

He hears gunfire. He touches her hand. 'There is fighting. We should go to our homes.'

She smiles and kisses his mouth. He realises they have never dared kiss in the light. 'Let us leave now while we still believe in lightness before the darkness enters the love that exists in our hearts.'

They hold hands and he walks her as close to her home as he dares without risking the eyes of anyone. She waves to him, she whispers goodbye.

He calls on God to protect her, to allow no harm to ever come to their love.

Zeinab cursed the day she met Omar and his family, cursed agreeing to marry him. When they weren't arguing, they disagreed, and on everything from where to place the matches to how to spend their money. They had money but it caused them so much trouble that she believed it better if they had been just as poor as everyone.

Take this business with the gift. It was for his sister's wedding which was to be next week. Who gets married when the villagers take their gunfights into the streets? Most of the time, the violence is elsewhere: in the mountains, in the city, in battles over the sea, but how are we to dance when it is possible we might be shot at when we step outside?

You are being dramatic. You exaggerate.

It made her so angry that he said this. Had it been her family, she would not have been so worried. They were not supplying arms, none were vocal about this side or that, but him, his lot, they carried weapons from the border in their fleet of trucks and he believed this made them immune rather than sitting ducks.

I do not wish to go. You go, if you will not listen to sense.

He told her to suit herself.

He did not buy his sister a gift. He put money into an envelope and she watched him lick it with his tongue and then seal it shut.

He has sealed our fate, just like that envelope.

He kissed the top of her head and went to the car.

She left the house with the kids to go to the park. She made up games about trees, she told them to run around and all the while her ears were listening far away.

When there was gunfire, she was not surprised and she told the children to not be afraid. Perhaps it was in the direction of the hall, perhaps it was not, but when there were more shots, she was certain it was to the east where only a few houses stood.

If he has died, we are ruined and I will not stay here another day.

Already she was thinking of the future, she was considering which was the best of the plans she had made. She was alone, she had the children and he had left them a violent ending, a lot of money and an easily targeted house.

She would leave. She did not need to be afraid. People did this all the time. Zeinab wished she could have locked him like a prisoner in their house, but he was so stubborn he would've broken out, called her silly and then continued along on his path.

She remembered how he liked to say *each person has their own path*.

What did a path mean if one was dead, if one did not live out a single day as a bride?

She could curse Omar, she could scream into the night, but there were the children to consider and already she mourns him, even without proof he has died. She knows it in her heart though: the violence in the direction of the hall and then towards their house.

What does it mean if a person is a success with money but too stupid to stay alive?

Perhaps he was better with money matters but Zeinab knew—and he had admitted it many times—that she trumped him in the ordinary matters of life.

The one with her baby stayed the longest. She was one of the first to arrive and the last to leave because she had nowhere else to go. She had few skills the world needed, no talents, nothing anyone could want except to sell the space between her legs and she was not going to stoop to that for money, not when there was a God above.

    He sees her around, this religious man, and she does not trust him, not with the stories that fill her head, but she decides to listen when he visits her with his wife and shows her the house his lover has left, promising to install her there with the lowest rent. The truth is she cannot pay the rent but he doesn't ask and the lover never returns and they agree she has abandoned this house and so you can say it all worked out for the best.

You are wasting your life.

The voice woke Fatima in the middle of the night.

That was all the voice said but she already knew what it meant.

Zaki left like many his age to seek his fortunes overseas. It had been two years and the war that they predicted would exhaust itself in the spring after he left was gaining momentum still. She did not base this judgement on the casualties which doubled each year, but on the news, the open threats of more strikes, more blood, more of the old *eye for an eye*.

It was picking up, not settling down, and two letters kept her hopeful despite the years.

When she read his letters, she whispered his words and she could hear them in Zaki's voice. He had promised to return and Zaki was a man of his word.

Her mother had been gentle and then increasingly aggressive as she continued to wait for Zaki's return.

'My daughter, he has left. Nothing but madness will convince him to return.'

But he told me he loved me before he left.

He had held her hand and then pressed it to his lips and she thought it was like a scene from a film.

She told no one about this and she kept secret the memory of his kiss.

You are wasting your youth, your beauty. You are wasting your days when you could have any man.

He had told her she was so beautiful and as soon as he could, he would return for her. It would take him a year or two to establish himself, to build up his money, to arrange a house, to send word to his parents to ask for her hand.

She pictured this day and although she would have liked them to be together to celebrate, she would say yes a million times over because already she could see their days together and the years ahead.

Fatima had read the two letters yesterday. They were the declarations of his care and affections, they were his promises for when they would be together at last.

She read them walking, she mouthed them as her father listened to the news on the radio and she felt so far from her mother who was counting the money their relatives had sent from overseas.

Their village was safe, and besides, if the fighting came closer, they could leave by the mountain road and stay with her mother's side until it settled down again.

You are wasting your life.

All day the voice drowned out the letters and by the end of the day, she could not remember Zaki's voice.

When her mother said *we need to leave*, Fatima gathered her things and at the last minute she left the letters behind.

She did not need to be sleeping to be woken by a voice that was clear.

The world had intervened in her plans with a simple message that could not be denied.

A simple message.
A single word.
Two letters.
Go.

I meant to stay, I meant to wait, but how can I justify waiting years based on two letters and a few memories? I waited at the start and I thought strong are those that wait without a word, without a sound, but I started to doubt the sanity of this choice. I was a young woman, you have to understand. I was a woman of my time and my place. You left me and you went far and what were my options but to wait or to look for love elsewhere?

I never doubted your love for me. It was never that. I wish for you to understand this. I waited three years, I waited till the roof had collapsed in and then I thought I cannot wait in this way as the country is beaten into the ground.

I had walked once, the first time, when we left for that mountain place, and I walked again when in the latest round the house was destroyed.

What comfort are memories when I am unsure if I shall live out the day? What comfort are written words when my family, so many of them, I did not know if they were dead or alive? What did it mean to me to wait in a time like this? You were living a life overseas, perhaps it was better, perhaps it was worse, there was no way for me to know.

He did not come to me with love even though there is much love in his heart. He came to me and he said we shall look after each other and I could think of nothing that could comfort me more.

You see our life. You see how bare it is. You can see the plainness of how we live but there is this affection between us and now we have these children and it is something I can touch every day. I shall not be left alone to worry in the night and I have more than the words of the past to comfort me.

He is a good man and we have a good life together and there is nothing I wish for or I feel that I need.

I am sorry that you return with your hope, that the place you find is not the one you left, that this young woman you made your promise to, she is no longer anywhere. I am sorry for you and I am sorry if you came on my account.

I hope you do not think to hurt me with your words because I could not keep a promise I did not understand. I hope we can keep our memories, that we can smile when we see each other, that the secrets of the past shall be kept safe in our hearts.

That is my hope, and I hope, Zaki, that you will understand.

He did not wish to hurt her because she had turned his world upside down.

He should have checked.

He should have asked.

He had assumed.

He had made a great mistake.

He looked at Fatima and knew the best thing he could do was to say goodbye and walk away.

He was going to fling himself into the well.

He was the stupidest person alive.

He was going to do it.

What would he tell his parents after he had promised them he planned on asking her to be his wife?

The years abroad had softened his mind. If Fatima had been their daughter, they would not have allowed her to wait the years for a man who may or may not come back.

Go to your life, they would have said, *go to your life. Do not waste it and wait.*

He was defeated. He stared at the sky, he stared at the sun, he stared and he could have cried.

Mustapha, an old friend from school, called out a hello and he joined him in the park, Mustapha talked, oblivious to how Zaki wished to die. Mustapha who invited him to dinner, who insisted, who reminded him it had been such a long time and asked what exactly brought you back?

Zaki began to cry and Mustapha told him what bothered him would pass, there was a God above, that they struggled together in these difficult times.

After he cried his tears and dried his eyes and told himself he would not think her name, he would leave her to the past, he told Mustapha, yes, he would come to dinner and they would play a hand of cards and if one ignored the world entirely, it would be as good as the times that had long ago passed.

The true story, the real story, is not the one they told. The story they told and agreed upon, that had settled into their hearts and minds, is different from the one whispered around the well.

The skeleton of their version went like this: an older man preyed on a younger woman, her family intervened, they married, it was the best arrangement for everyone.

That is the version they like, that makes the story neater than it really is.

Consider this: Abu Bakr had a farm that had many fruit trees and fields of vegetables too. When the war started—and no one could point to its precise start . . . there's fighting, there's more fighting, oh, it looks like there's a war—the neighbours were working in the city, they were tending their own fields, the men were driving trucks to Turkey, Russia, occasionally one claimed to have reached as far as France. Abu Bakr could not drive and he did not wish to learn as there was nowhere he wished to go that was not accessible by buses, and while Um Bakr told him repeatedly the benefits of a car, he was not convinced.

Cars suffered car trouble. They relied on fuel. The situation of the country was precarious. A donkey, a bicycle, a set of feet were more reliable than an engine that depended on shipments of fuel trickling into their village.

He hired workers, among them the children of his neighbours. His only requirement was that they worked hard for a full day.

Abu Bakr gave Noura work because she was young and she needed the money to establish her life. He had daughters her age and he was conscious that Noura did not have the money of her parents to fall back on like his girls and that she would need money of her own.

She reminded him of himself at her age. He once laughed a lot, he was known for his jokes, but age had taken both his strength and his wit. Um Bakr was fond of reminding him of his past, how once he was the life of any gathering and now she needed a tractor to drag him out the door.

He protested. Um Bakr was being dramatic. *Come on, it is not like that, I am not that bad*, but when he saw Noura, he was reminded of being young again.

He will tell later of the distance he kept, of how he was conscious of God, that he was a praying man, that she would brush against him in the field and it took him weeks to admit her actions were deliberate.

Even when he was sure, he doubted, because he could not understand why. He was grey, his teeth were yellow, she could click her fingers and the best of the young would run to her. He had seen it with his own eyes, he had seen her tongue rip apart a worker who had tried to make a joke at her expense.

It did not matter what he said. It did not matter how good a man he was known to be. What people remembered were her brothers coming with their axes and sticks, a neighbour bringing a gun, to demand he marry Noura after he'd had his way with her.

A wealthy girl would not have been in the situation of needing work to have enough to eat.

A wealthy girl could have been checked by doctors and still have her life ahead of her.

A wealthy girl could have taken her money and reinvented herself overseas but a poor girl like Noura was married off to him and he believed it had been her plot all along.

He built her a small house at the other end of the fields and even though he never visited his second wife, Um Bakr never forgave him, not with the facts clear as day. She never forgave him even though the other one never gave birth to a child (further evidence in his defence), he kept his distance, and their only interaction was the amount of money he gave her monthly so she had enough to eat.

He need not have worried about her.

She had landed herself the biggest fish she could and now she washed her hands of him. If she had men visit her, he had no idea and he did not care. His name was tainted, hers was clear, and with the years her tongue became longer while Abu Bakr became more and more thin.

Mahmoud and SooSoo had been married a week and he did not know what to do with her. She seemed to him a different person. Once she had been vibrant, a joker, and now she barely said a word. She fixed their breakfast, waving away his attempts to help, and placed it before him as if he were a stranger in a restaurant. Then she sat opposite him sullenly, drinking her tea like she was being forced.

She used to laugh. She had a nice smile. It was what first caught his eye.

She once told him what she wanted and there was nothing he left undone. Nothing. She would say *I need this* and he would bring it to her. *We are out of this* and he'd go instantly so she would not be without. *This is old* and, without a word, that same day he had it replaced.

He did everything for her and all he wanted was for SooSoo to smile, but she sat before him, as silent as the dead.

He left for work and he thought about her as he walked away. Had he said something, had someone slighted her, had there been an injury to her pride? He thought to address it openly with her but his experience told him that this would make her withdraw and hide. Or else there was the possibility of denial.

He did not know who he could ask. The men he knew would shrug their shoulders, open their hands, look to the skies. *The mysteries, this is God's work.* If he asked his mother, a cousin, SooSoo would never forgive him. It would be a betrayal to go to her friends or anyone on her side, and because there was no one else left, he went to her mother and asked for help.

SooSoo's mother came around with cleaning supplies, with a food basket and five types of mops. She dragged SooSoo by her arm and sat her on the couch and proceeded to clean around her daughter in silence. Perhaps they had perfected a method of communication using blinks.

SooSoo stretched out on the sofa and he could not believe his eyes when she began to cry. Her mother put out plate of food and ordered her to eat.

He went outside but he did not go far enough. Always he would remember SooSoo's tears and her saying, 'This is not the life I want.'

Her mother's answer was too low for him to make out but he cursed himself for listening to their conversation, for hearing what was not meant for his ears, but now that he had heard it, it hurt him as if she had said it to him directly.

It hurt him especially because he intended to worship the ground beneath her feet.

It hurt him especially because he was attentive to her every whim.

It hurt him especially because she was allowed her tears but he was forced from their house to give her privacy.

It hurt him, it hurt him, it would always hurt him, and he could not mention it or clarify it with her.

In the future, they would argue openly and so many times he wanted to throw her line into the argument, to demand she explain herself, but there was a presence at his shoulder who told him to step away when he had this urge. And he would leave it by biting his tongue, by walking from the room, by asking her to talk later when he was in a calmer frame of mind.

It bothered him for years and he wished to ask her when they were happy and smiling, years later when their kids were big and grown, but he couldn't, or perhaps his angel prevented him and instead he walked away.

He could not ask anyone except for her mother and so he went to her one day after they had argued and he despaired about her, him, their marriage, and everything else including the state of the world.

Her mother listened patiently, put tea before him, urged him to have some sweets.

He was almost in tears so he drank his tea, ate his sweets and thanked her for being his mother-in-law.

Before he left, she touched his arm and said, 'That day we spoke, those were private words. I told her that you're a kind man, that you're a good man, that your marriage will be many happy years. SooSoo, she was upset that day but when I went to leave, as you go to leave now, she told me *mother, you are right and together, no matter the circumstances of the world, we will have happy years.*'

Mahmoud left quickly without a goodbye because he was about to cry. He arrived home and kissed SooSoo hello.

All these years they had lived happily and he had been oblivious and tormented by private words.

People come here to throw themselves in the well. Sometimes it's an accident but most of the time it's not.

For example:
The boy who climbs into the well on a dare and then pretends to be stuck to frighten his friends. Or the one who slips over after losing her son and her family says it was an accident but the truth is it was not. Or the one who climbs in for some peace because she has grown tired of the town and its talk and what was happening abroad and then in their city.

The last one fell into the well because of her inability to reconcile beauty and the world. *You see, I am religious and I wish to pray but then I marvel at the world. I am distracted by the colours as if under a spell and that makes me forget all my prayers. I generalise* (she paced at this), *I generalise about what has troubled me these years but how do I attend to the beauty when there is so much fighting, so much warring, and tomorrow the world may end?*

She could not balance this one and when they fished her out, they called it an accident, ignoring the increase in accidents as of late.

The water is still, the night is quiet, and there is no creature moving that my ears can hear.

As it is time for their peace, it is also the same for mine.

I live here, I rest here and sometimes I sleep, but I am now filled with a spirit sickness at the ending to their lives that I am forced to see.

The three wise men meet later at the well to congratulate themselves.

They spoke of their day and this is the story that I heard.

Risen in our midst is a girl who dares to raise an instrument to her mouth. It is a traditional instrument and it is wooden and doesn't she know it is only used by men?

The wise asked among the neighbours if anyone thought the girl was not right in the head. Perhaps she could be forgiven her simplicity and a caring aunt could hold her hand and say *no more of this, my dear.*

It was a pity because the reports came back saying one story, that there was nothing wrong with the girl. An uncle had asked her what possessed her to do such a thing, taking a musical instrument to her lips.

The girl did not know of the traditions around flutes, the rules that said others were allowed but she was not, so when her uncle asked, she responded truthfully because, remember, she is a little girl.

A committee of the concerned discussed the traditions, they made lists to present so that she and those like her would never be tempted again.

They presented the lists and the girl cried and her parents were convinced by the verses the committee had assembled and then they played so their message was heard.

We did not know about the rules, we did not know it was an affront to decency and our faith and whatever else, our girl is innocent and she did not know that she had erred.

The three wise men congratulate themselves.

Imagine a girl putting a long, rounded object between her lips and men thinking of music and nothing else.

The crisis has been averted, they have heard the verses and no one can argue with what the wise have said.

CHILDREN OF THE SUN

Abu Bakr, when he thought of his son, always remembered him in the sun. They were children in those days—him as much as them—and entire days would be spent at the beach. He would joke with the boy and call him *my little shark*. It has been years since he thought of those days and how once he did not need to rely on memory to see his son alive.

Um Talal, she used to hit her daughter to make her behave, but she gave up later because the girl was wild. She was so wild that she ran away from home, picked up a gun and did not part from it until she died. They brought her daughter back, and she remembered the one time she put on a dress by herself. Those days belonged to history and the dress now sits in a box in a cupboard. None knows of its existence except Um Talal who takes it out and looks at it and thinks of the times she pushed the girl into dresses, and how this dress is the only thing left of her daughter that she can still touch.

Um Jihad, her only son was named after her father-in-law and she thinks now there is no worse way to curse a child. Jihad was a slow boy but he always had a smile. His death was an accident and his cousin took the blame, but what good is that to her now that her child is in the ground?

Abu Omar, he remembers the day his two eldest had been determined to get to the mountaintop. 'It has been a shadow on our lives but today nothing will stop us scaling its heights.' Their mother had told them to watch their words, that such words could be interpreted as a direct challenge to God. The children laughed at this but he did not because he had seen before how God worked.

Um Kamel, her main regret was telling him he had the face of a rat. The minute she said it, she regretted it and she wondered about her only child carrying that comment around his entire life. She should have told him she loved him, that she counted it the happiest day in her life when God had blessed her with a child. *After you were born was the best time in my life. Before that I had lived in darkness, and after I had you I thought how did I not notice the sun before?* He never mentioned the rat, that she had said his face was pointy and his ears stuck out. Her husband, not the boy's father, told her she had made a mistake, and she wondered if Omar thought of her words, if they were the last memory he had in the moment she later heard of that had made her world so black.

They come here, these ones, they unburden themselves in this little park. Some peer into the darkness, some look into the well, some call out, some wipe tears from their eyes. There is something about this park, and my presence, that makes them remember their children and believe they have not yet departed from this life.

WOMAN UNDONE

We are to make it through this night and then another day will begin.
Salma was tired of the senseless commentary. People's predictions had no foundation. They were slapped together from what they had overheard.

The war will end tomorrow.
                        The war will go on for the rest of our lives.
We will die tonight.
                        Our death will happen when God says.
We all need to make an effort.
                        It is an impossible task
                        no matter how hopeful we are.
We are all of us doomed.
                        We are all of us saved.

She tried to listen but she had no more time and she was on her way out.
When the first bomb landed, she took the flashlight, the bag of bread, she checked the water and she sat in the chair downstairs.

She thought she would read the paper but she was too rattled in the fragments between the shelling of the town.

She began a list the way another person might begin to pray.

First she was going to cut her hair. It had been years but it was an indulgence she could not overlook.

She was going to have ice cream by the sea as she had done with her family. It was the seven of them and they had done the trip once and it lived as her most vivid memory.

She was going to re-enrol at the university, if the university was still standing after this night was through.

She could not think *if I make it through*. She was going to make it through. She was counting on making it through as if it were part of God's big plan.

She was going to clear around the well. She was going to enlist the townspeople to paint the benches so they could have a place of beauty again.

How exactly was she going to afford the paint . . . who was going to help her . . . what if they tore up her plans . . .

She was not going to think of that. She was going to make it through the night because there was work to do, hopes to fulfil, there was still so much to learn, see and eat.

There was still so much, and if she was patient and if she hoped and if she counted, God would take care of the rest and see them through the night so that their lives could resume.

THE DOUBLE

Salma had a double that had taken over her life.

Consider: the war had ended thirty-three years ago but she still woke in the early hours of the morning and listened for explosives going off. Were they close, were they far, was it the capital, was it a neighbouring town?

There was only the sound of a truck's engine and then the bark of a dog. The wind moved through the trees and from the books she read she knew this was meant to be peaceful, but she had learned the wind could as easily conceal the enemy's approach.

No one liked to talk in terms of the enemy anymore.

We are all friends. See us on TV, we are shaking hands. I have butchered your friends, you have decimated the places I have known, but we shake hands and it is water under the bridge.

So many peace deals had been signed.

Look at us smiling, look at us standing before our flags, our patriotism no barrier to us around the table as we engage in friendly, modern talk.

These tabled gatherings were the stills in the newspaper and on the TV, and the townspeople talked of the extended debates they had watched.

She counted it still in terms of enemies and friends, of *our side and theirs*. The wars of the past could not be erased with the peaceful symbol of a handshake, of flags that filled the screen.

Once she had believed in her life, she had believed in a dream, but at some point, her double had taken over the reins and the other Salma retreated to a fictional land of poems and music while the double tracked the guns and the bombs. The double had a legendary appetite for these details and she had amassed a formidable treasure trove.

What happened to the woman dreaming of ice cream, what happened to learning and bettering one's life?

All she knew was that she would hear the wind and think of the enemy's steps, she would hear the quiet and think *silence, how well you conceal the knife.*

FRIENDS

Someone had pushed the great pause button on her life. Someone had rewound the tape. Salma did not see the present. Salma saw the world in the past.

Her friend asked her *have you seen the new cafe?* and she described its location using a pen and paper to make sure they both understood the precise location she was talking about.

Salma shook her head. *That was a clothes store when I went to town the other day.*

This friend was new and inclined to hear Salma's version out and doubt her own. *What other memories of mine have been compromised, what else have I got wrong?*

This friend—the new friend—did not remain a friend for long because she checked the location (it *was* a cafe) and she wanted to break into Salma's place and demand that she see that it was a cafe with her own eyes.

They had the argument but the friend gave up because Salma's involvement was vague. She started sentences, she left them half-finished, she shook herself and said *where was I?* before going off on a tangent.

The friend shook her head. Either Salma was a liar or she was fuddled and unreliable. Either way, Salma was not someone the friend wanted in her life.

In their last conversation before they permanently parted ways, Salma monologued and the friend—the new friend, the no-longer-a-friend—slowly backed away.

I am sometimes stuck in the past.

There has been a pause button on my life.

A double is living my life.

I hear bombs in the night. Other times I wait for them to go off.

I had a look the other day. It is a clothing store, not a cafe.

Someone has stuffed cotton between my ears.

Some days I see myself dissolving and I am a puddle of water on the ground.

I am trying, I am trying, I have been trying all my life.

I have been condemned. My mind is forever in the past.

For ten years I have been meaning to fix the broken glass in the wall outside but, whether I fix it or I don't, who exactly cares? I can't imagine God's going to be asking about the glass on Judgement Day.

The former friend left and tried to rid Salma's words from her head. The lines echoed, chased each other, ate each other's ends, but she kept walking till she found the place, the one whose location they had agreed on after drawing the map.

The argument could end . . . it was ended . . . enough.

That was no clothes store. *People do not drink coffee between racks of garments, Salma. They only do that in cafes.*

THE CARD PLAYERS

The men were serious card players and Salma thought *I will start my own group*. They could meet in the living area and eat their snacks and play a round of cards. It would be a friendly way to pass the time, it would be a suitable way for them to relax.

The women she contacted were enthusiastic. They told Salma they were excited about the impending evening and insisted on bringing snacks.

Just come along. There is no need for anything. I have everything here already.

They came along but they ignored what she said.

Amal brought her teething baby who the neighbours had threatened to throw off a balcony.

Maysa brought a sad story that she tried to cover with laughter but which made them all end up in tears.

Lubna brought her argileh that they refused to smoke at first but then they gave in and laughed because they wished it was hashish.

Reem brought her back pain for which no amount of cushions could provide relief.

Lubna pointed to the cards, Maysa made the coffee, Amal patted the baby who was almost asleep and Reem said, 'Shall we begin?'

They went through the motions of playing but once the game was up, Lubna collected the cards and put them away and said, 'It's nice to have this time together.'

They smiled and said they agreed.

They repeated the gathering weekly: an evening, most of them turning up regularly, the cards never seen again.

IN THIS LIFE

None of the women in Salma's family had been to school. Her mother, though she believed education important, had never set foot in a classroom and when discussing her childhood, Salma's mother began her stories with, 'If I could go back.'

Salma's maternal aunt once said education was a waste of time but later in life she changed her mind. Salma remembered Aunt Rawa putting out a cigarette and saying, 'Maybe if I had got an education, I wouldn't need people to read things for me all the time.'

Um Talal, her father's sister, made no secret of her displeasure at the state of the education provided. *Education should be free, schools should be free and available for everyone. God did not mean for humans to spend their lives like dumb beasts.*

Salma's other aunt was Lulu, the one no one ever mentioned. Lulu was still alive and she had gone overseas but no one knew the details of how. There was a story that she had bribed an overseas man to pretend she was his wife and that was how she had managed her escape from this place. But the numbers did not add up, especially the matter of the bribe or how Lulu had managed the cost of a ticket and passport or how she later came to own a house. Defending Lulu was no use because then the defender would be tainted with the same brush. Salma knew that when Lulu was mentioned, she should just let the talk play out and do her best to keep her mouth shut.

Salma had a sister but her memories of her were patchy and needed photos to refresh them. There were only three photos of Rajaa and she was smiling in all of them, her hair pinned up in a special style for a wedding in the one that Salma liked the most. Rajaa never made it to school and it was a subject that their parents had fought ferociously about, with the fights often ending in nails and blood. When Salma thought about her sister, she had no memories of how Rajaa had spent her time. Perhaps she swept inside, perhaps she visited people, chatting and carrying information like a messenger bird from house to house. Perhaps she knitted and sewed, perhaps she listened to the news of the world. Salma made up stories about how Rajaa had spent her time but even she knew these were not memories and her speculation was founded on imagination alone.

When she went to school for the very first time, Salma stepped in with the presence of the women on both sides of her family. They spoke in her ear and she tried to get them to be quiet, and Salma sat straight in class, prepared and alert for the teacher's first line.

Rajaa was silent and the others spoke loudly and later Salma realised that this was the only way the others could get an education in this life.

THEN SHE WORKED

Out of the five of them, Amal had least wanted to work. Her husband encouraged her desire for idleness, and besides, their three children were a job and it was enough for her to turn her attention to them. Amal's mother had different ideas that she broadcast around their village day and night at the top of her lungs. 'She is becoming lazy. Soon she'll be bigger than an elephant and unable to move, and Rafaat encourages her because that way she stays the centre of his world.'

No one said it but of course Amal's mother would think like that. She had buried two husbands and, in her sixties, rumour had it she was looking for a third. She had a house, she had two apartments she let out and she never left the house unless her hair was perfectly in place. The young men joked when they saw her walking up the street. 'This one finds a bed for the men she has. First there's the one she sleeps in but then she finds them an eternal one in the ground.' But Amal had listened to her mother's words her entire life and she had resisted by marrying a man her mother did not like, a small satisfaction considering the days of her life stretched out emptily and there was nothing much to look forward to on the horizon.

The job, when she got it, was as a teacher in a school. It provided money for her clothes and enough to fix up their house and fill it with pretty things. She first replaced the curtains with bright red ones that Rafaat said might lead observers to mistake the house for one hosting ladies of the night. Amal ignored him and kept the curtains and it did not matter how much people nudged each other as they passed their house. She bought paint in three colours and ordered their boys onto ladders to paint the walls yellow and awnings white, and then the balcony railings and window frames in blue. Rafaat saw it and said, 'Now we live in a circus house.'

Amal ignored him and she ignored the boys who questioned the colour scheme and whether it made their house stand out too much.

With her work, Amal became slimmer, she dressed better and her mother said, 'Anyone can now easily see that Amal is my girl.'

Rafaat was annoyed when Amal said she was going to buy a house. It was not necessary, they had a roof over their heads, was she going to be an accumulator of wealth? She barely heard him and she was already plotting ahead and whenever the jokes became too much, she went to her mother and to Salma because these two would at least understand.

Salma said, 'You need something of your own.'

Her mother said, 'Look straight ahead. Don't listen to the people standing on the sides.'

That night, Amal lay in their bed, Rafaat asleep at her side, and she realised that while her days had once been identical and fashioned on a production line, her life now had possibilities.

Salma remembered when Maysa asked Amal if she could have a room in the house, that she needed it for a while because Maysa's family was threatening to throw her out if she persisted with her plans.

And there was Reem who had married Omar, neither trusting his parents enough to live with them.

Then there was Amal herself who sometimes went to the top room and collapsed on the bed she kept and listened to the ocean undisturbed, wondering if she would ever move again. It had been another difficult day at work and she knew she should go home but she called Rafaat and told him she could not move and she was going to have a piece of bread and then go to sleep. He said nothing except to tell her to make sure she came home the next day. She listened to him and when she arrived home from work, he said to her, 'You work too hard.'

She dismissed his words but this time he insisted and so Amal said, 'I would not have it any other way. I have a world to myself.'

'You are your mother's daughter,' he said, and she knew he meant it as an insult.

She held her head in her hands. 'What would make a difference is having some help at home.'

He looked at her and she looked at him. Rafaat was the first to look away but that meant nothing after all these years. There would be many more years to come and they would have to make their days easier in a way that did not leave their lives worse than how they had once been. He wondered if this would end with Amal leaving him.

So Rafaat found a woman to do the housework and the cooking, and Amal watched this woman who swept the floor daily, who wiped at the tiles with a cloth. She watched her washing plates, bringing in the vegetables and fruit and cutting up both into snacks that she presented on plates. Some days, Amal left this house and went to the other house and climbed the stairs to the third floor where she had her bedroom, where she could see the sea through the window if she lay on her side. Rafaat had asked for a key but she said no and he turned away and shrugged.

She wondered about the future. She wondered if it would become too hard and they would each go their own way or if they would have this space between them and live their lives in parallel or if it was even worth thinking about? It was better to listen to the sea and the silence in the house and when she was ready, she could finally get some rest.

DOORWAY OPENINGS

It was a habit Salma developed early in her life. She had learned it from a cowboy movie. She sat always with her chair facing the door so she could see who was entering and who was leaving. She did this out in cafes, in the classroom, she did this when she visited friends and when she was alone at home. When she sat down to her meals, she moved the chair so that the window was at her side and she could see the door when she lifted her eyes.

It was a habit uninterrogated that she kept for the rest of her life. She only became aware of it in her forties when Amal asked her why she sat in the same spot, if she was waiting for someone, if she was even aware of what she did.

Salma gave her the long version of the story about how cowboys kept a wall at their back and watched doorways to detect threats entering the room. Amal asked *what threats?* and Salma just shrugged because she had no answer and she was no longer sure what she even meant.

She noticed it then. It was in her memories as well. In her school days, she had chosen the chair at the far wall to see immediately who entered the classroom. At home, her favourite lounge was not the one that faced the TV but the solitary one angled towards the entrance point. Even when she had her coffee on the roof, she did not face the sea even though it was a view she loved. She did not face the mountain which she could outline when she closed her eyes. She faced the stairwell, the most logical entrance to the roof.

Logic could not argue the point that threats could come from above, that with no barriers between her and the sky, she was exposed to what the world chose to rain upon her head.

That was the logic but the reality was she knew more stories about killers entering from a doorway or a window than up above. It did not matter. She could not quiet this fear and so she kept watching doorways till her life's very end.

HELICOPTER STORIES

All day there had been helicopters in the sky. They hung low over their town and the sound of them was still there at night.

They speculated about the helicopters. They were watching, they were waiting, they were on their way south. The news mentioned them, of course, that these were frightened helicopters, but that is not how Salma read their movement in the sky. They were waiting, they were waiting for the right time.

The first day the helicopters were a bother, but on the second they were background noise and people came out of their houses. Amal and Lubna agreed that their emergence was what the helicopters wanted but Salma was not so sure. She thought about them at night-time which was easy because they were hovering above her house. They were distant, they were close, and as she became sleepy, she imagined each helicopter had its individual sound.

The third day was strike day and they expected it but still they were terrified. Seven families lost their homes. Not a single person died because everyone happened to be outside. Lubna said it was a miracle but Salma thought one of them must have known and was therefore likely to be a spy.

The helicopters were busy in the week ahead and Salma spent entire days in the bottom of her house. She thought putting her hands over her ears would help but sometimes she could feel the vibrations in her heart. She drank water, she sat in darkness and she thought *this is like the revelation cave, and when I begin to hear voices, I will know it is madness and I have lost my mind.*

There were many helicopter theories patched together from what each person heard and what each person said. Every person had a helicopter story, and Salma had no real story about helicopters but she liked listening to these stories in the decades to come. One time she was asked for her story and for once she broke her silence. 'All these helicopter stories but I want to return to the time of the birds.'

THE SEA

For ten days she has been meaning to go to the beach. And the beach is only a hundred metres away.

Each morning she wakes, Salma thinks *this is another day I did not go to the beach.*

Dissatisfaction clings to her throughout the day. The house does not look right, the colour of the mountain is duller than it has been in the past. All her things appear frayed and worn and she moves with the sense that she has taken a tumble in life.

Ten days.

Then eleven.

Then she loses count and thinks *it has been a month.*

The sea is so close and it has begun to appear in my dreams.

Finally she goes, irritable, *what exactly is the fuss?*

She sees the sea that is the ocean that is the endlessness of the sky above. She sees the world here and it operates at a different pace.

At first she berates herself for leaving it so long.

Then she thinks *relax, you are here now.*

Finally she is at peace and she feels the sea has carved out a space in her insides and that she can breathe and be alive.

Then it is time to turn and to promise herself that she will not leave it so long until next time.

THE FISHERMAN AND THE SEA

Salma found the net at her cousin's house. It sat in a heap in the corner and every day her cousin said he meant to get rid of it. Years she listened to this plan and one day she decided to take the net off his hands. He insisted he would have someone drop it off to save her carrying it in the streets.

She protested, he protested, eventually she relented and her cousin carried the net over in a sack.

It sat next to the well and everyone commented that it would be best used as fuel for fire when they next burned their waste. Every day she watched the fishermen, every day her head was filled with ideas that she kept to herself lest someone talk the life out of them.

She took up walking the short ten minutes to the beach to see how they cast their net. From the shore it seemed a straightforward task. Most worked in pairs or they brought a child with them and she did think about asking for help but she worried about an idea and its life.

The night before she took the net down to the sea, she wondered if she needed to know how to properly swim. Surely she could walk it in until the water was up to her neck and then collect it later closer to sunset.

She slept and dreamed of the sea, and every time she set the net, a wave would knock her off her feet and she only stopped drowning when she woke.

Salma did not care if she drowned. Those were dreams and they had no power to harm her in the morning light. She took the net and dragged it behind her, already planning a spot to hide it close to the shore if what she caught today made it worthwhile to repeat the trip tomorrow.

There were many men on the beach in their shorts, with their line, with their nets, and a couple had the advantage of a boat.

She watched the man to her right with his two boys, and as they did, she copied what they did. Another man called to her and she thought he was telling her to stop, and then the man with his children sent one of his boys to help her set the net in a better spot for her catch.

The shouting grew louder and there was Abu Kamel yelling that this was his spot and how dare she come in with her net.

The net had been set and she would have retrieved it but the boy said to Abu Kamel, 'I did not know that the sea belonged to your dad.'

Abu Kamel lunged at the boy, whose name she later learned was Ahmed, and perhaps he would have hit him except Abu Ahmed called to his son and said, 'Come give me a hand.'

The boy left and Abu Kamel dropped his eyes, muttering about people who did not know their place.

Her catch was modest: five decent fish and two fish that were all bones and a waste of effort for the person who tried to eat them.

She did not think fishing was worth a second try but the next morning Ahmed knocked on her door. Abu Ahmed was waiting at a distance and Um Ahmed was yawning at his side. They walked together to the beach and Abu Ahmed said to her, 'I shall show you what I know.'

Salma told him that she was not going to fish again but she would come along with them to keep Um Ahmed company and to enjoy the peace of the morning sea.

Ahmed—how old was this boy?—said to her seriously *the sea is an angel and you cannot count your fortunes after you have fished it only once and so you will have to try again.* Listening to him, she could hear he was repeating words he had heard, and when his father hugged him, she understood the source.

Salma meant to sit with Um Ahmed but she insisted Salma go into the sea and learn how to fish so that at the very least she could always feed herself.

Later she invited them to her house to eat the fish she had caught the day before. They came in after her and Ahmed studied her knives and took the best one to clean the fish while Abu Ahmed supervised.

At the end of the lunch, Um Ahmed leaned back and said that it was the best meal she'd had in years.

The next day a religious man and his wife came to see Salma and they discussed fishing and how one could judge how favoured they were by God by the number of fish they brought home.

The man asked Salma how many fish she had caught on her first and second day, and she responded five and nine.

He shook his head and his wife said, 'It is plain to see that it is best you give up this fishing now. Men have an advantage and this is their task and if God meant for women to fish, then it would be women every morning to sea.'

She thought to burn their coffee, she thought to add chilli to the sweets, but she did not, and she kept the smile on her face as she nodded politely until they left.

The next day she did not go to the sea, the next day she did not move from her house, the next day Um Ahmed came to her house banging on the front door, threatening to break the windows if Salma did not let her in.

She finally opened the door in her house clothes and Abu Ahmed turned away when he saw how she was dressed. He took the children and walked away, calling that he would return in half an hour.

Um Ahmed walked into the kitchen and made the tea as if she was ready to kick something. She grabbed Salma's face and squeezed with two hands and then shook her by the shoulders. 'Are you going to let them tell you who can use the sea? If one can learn, one should learn, and if one has a skill, one should use it too. They come here with their religion but they grab an idea by its rear and you should know better than to trust religion like this. Today you fish, tomorrow perhaps you can help someone who has nothing to eat. Do you now mean to be stupid when you know better than this man with his very large beard?'

Salma said it had nothing to do with the visit, that she was tired, but Um Ahmed kicked at her foot and after that she was silent, and they sat like that until Abu Ahmed returned with the children. That evening Um Ahmed insisted that Salma have half the fish and when her husband was far away, she whispered she would continue to do this every day unless Salma went to fish.

The next day, Salma woke at dawn and took the net with her and she has been fishing ever since.

THE PLAN FOR THE DAY

This is later in her life. Her days have been spent in this village and she decides to take a drive. Her cousin says the car's engine is no good, that in the year ahead she should replace the car, but she has heard this advice for the past ten years, and besides, she has neither the money nor the energy to replace the tyres let alone an entire car. *It will have to keep running*, and just like her, the car has no other choice.

She leaves the house at dawn and it takes her three hours to reach the city in the north. She stops three times and has not yet made up her mind on where she is going today.

She counts the stops. The first time had been for breakfast, the second for fuel, the third she had seen a coffee stand. She was served Nescafé by a child who was ten, who whistled as he stirred the sugar, who asked her questions about her day ahead. She sees her life through his eyes for a moment and she admits it looks good from the outside. She has her car and she is driving and she can take her time and her general destination is the south. She gives him a tip and the boy smiles and tells her to look after herself.

The fourth stop is not necessary but she parks and she gets out of the car, her eyes sweeping back and forth across the water which glitters now that the sun has shown her face.

This is water to dive into. This is the sea from a film and she wants to hold it and fill her eyes with it, but no matter how she studies it, she cannot take it in, so she returns to her car, thinking about this impossibility.

Do others see the sea and feel their heart expand? Do their worries depart? In their life is there suddenly a sense of space where before they had been trapped?

Do others go for drives alone in a country where people travel in pairs, groups, the whole extended family?

Do others set off south with no destination, thinking to make it up as they go along, which she does out of necessity even though she cannot say it increases her peace?

She fills up at a petrol station and a youth wipes the windscreen. He makes a comment about the tyres which she ignores and he mentions a ruin that no one really goes to because it is overgrown with grass and trees. She asks for directions because it gives her a place to go and better if it is a place she has never seen. The youth writes instructions and she is aware of him standing against the wall, cursing the pen when it stops and then again when it punctures the paper.

'If you are going to the trouble of going there, there is an ice cream place and you must make a stop. Ask for Hala. She is my sister and tell her you have been sent by Bashir. She can tell you a few other places you must see and the villages nearby are at their prettiest this time of year.'

She thanks Bashir and studies the instructions he has given her. She can feel the day gaining definition and she can hear herself later telling this story, delivering it so that the listener would understand just how carefully intended her entire journey had been.

THE TIME I WENT OVERSEAS

The time Salma went overseas was forever referred to as *the time I went overseas*. The more Salma thought about her time overseas, the more it became mythical and she struggled to separate the facts from the natural distortions of memory.

For the record, the time she went overseas was a time in the past thirty years. It cost her the savings of three years and she did it once and she never went again. She went with her friend for a month, and Salma was convinced the colours had been sharper in the place overseas, that they became even brighter with the passing years.

The time I went overseas . . .

My month overseas . . .

When I was in that country overseas . . .

When these words left Salma's mouth, her friends knew that it would be a story they had heard till they knew it by heart, that sometimes they heard Salma deliver these lines in their dreams.

Her version of the trip diverged from Zahra's who had also gone on the same trip. Zahra would whisper to them afterwards *but this is how it really was,* and they learned to balance Salma's version with Zahra's, and if they had to choose a version, they would have said Zahra's had greater credibility. They based their judgement not on the history of the truth-telling of both women but on how much Salma reached for this trip more and more, while the only time Zahra mentioned it was to verify or revise the way Salma presented what had happened overseas.

Once Dunya asked Salma why she still spoke about the time overseas, why she brought it up every time, and Salma denied she mentioned it all the time, and they were all silent and avoided each other's eyes, and even Zahra was silent, believing it not the time to contradict what Salma had said about their time overseas.

Salma paced around the well and had conversations with Dunya that were listened to by the presence in the well who knew about that time overseas, as they all did, who got to know better that trip with the passing of the years.

Once Zahra claimed the wall in their hotel had been yellow while Salma was certain it had been red but there were no photos so the listeners were not sure if the wall had been red or yellow, but they did not believe Salma no matter how many times she insisted it had been red.

But it was red, I swear it was red. How can one not tell the difference between yellow and red? And there was that time she mistook that yellow for a white, and if you asked her friends, they would have said that Salma always had trouble with her eyes but she refused to get them checked.

Quietly they agreed between them to test Salma and Zahra on the colours to see if there was a difference between their perceptions, and they repeated this many times but they themselves couldn't agree on the colours and they decided to stop because the colours were causing them to disagree.

Salma knew they wanted her to stop telling her story, to pretend that the time she had been overseas did not exist but she refused to do this because she had been overseas and she had every right to talk about that time as much as she pleased.

And she knew the wall was red, not yellow, because she went back to her memories again and again and she repeated the time she was overseas in her head and she had no doubt about any of the details, while Zahra didn't do that so no wonder she couldn't remember a red from a yellow, and hadn't she in fact drifted aimlessly that time they were overseas?

DESTINED FOR GREATNESS

What Salma disliked about Dawood was not that he was young and silly but that he thought he was great. The first two were forgivable but each time she listened to her nephew speak, she thought *here we go again*.

When she told Amal about Dawood, Amal just shook her head. 'The problem is not Dawood but your brother raising him so he has a big head.'

Dawood had played football since he was ten and the way his father spoke about his skill, you'd think he believed Dawood was destined for the World Cup. On his eleventh birthday, Dawood announced that he hated football and would prefer to spend the summer swimming with his friends.

While Dawood was good at school, their village was a small pond and what did it mean if he topped the grade out of a pool of thirteen? *He is the smartest, he is the brightest, one day he will be a surgeon of the brain or one of those people who can capture the energy of the sun and wind.*

Every time she walked past the shop where Dawood worked, she remembered how her brother meant for the boy to be a surgeon or engineer. Every time she spoke to Dawood, he spoke of the future and where he was going and how it was going to work out this time. She had heard the story so many times that she wanted to shake Dawood and say *enough's enough*.

She was there the time the neighbour said to him *enough's enough* and she had believed it was something that would make her laugh but upon hearing it, the words made her want to cry.

Dawood fell silent and he did not say another word for the rest of the night. He said his goodbyes politely but the smile was gone entirely from his face.

He stopped talking of his plans after that and Salma's brother spoke of them more as if to compensate. Whenever she went past the shop, she imagined Dawood going about his ordinary day. Once he had his dream and his hope but now he was going nowhere just like everyone.

IN HER HEAD

Every night when she goes to sleep, Salma begins to count the dead. They appear in her dreams and through the years she has come to expect them.

Amal says she, Salma, has no claim to the dead, that she is not even related to them, that she is inserting herself into a story that has nothing to do with her. But this does not stop the dead from their nightly visits and Salma resigning herself to them even though she prefers to dream of sunshine and spaces of open air.

The dead arrive in hordes, in waves, they move in a strict military line. Each face is distinct and Salma knows their names and she makes sure to use their names when addressing them.

When Amal asks her about the dreams, about what happens nightly, Salma gives a vague answer that Amal now expects.

I mean, they just arrive. Sometimes we're here, she waves her arm at the house, the village, the sweep taking in the sea, *sometimes we're in places I don't know. Maybe I picked those places from the TV.*

Amal insists that this is further evidence that these dead do not belong to Salma, that by talking about these dreams she is claiming a story that is not really hers.

Salma is not sure if the dead are hers or if she is even trying to claim them. Most nights, she sleeps as if she's collapsing and she wakes as if she's had no rest.

Perhaps by mentioning the dead she is claiming them but she only speaks of them because it is now thirty years and she still sees them.

There are the three sisters that died whose faces she saw on the TV.

There is the man who was found murdered and buried in a shallow garden bed.

There is the baby that was drowned and caught in a net like a fish in the sea.

There is the old lady at the foot of the building who could buy bread only on the days she begged.

There are the buried who have been dead thirty years and there are others whose bodies were never found and so their spirits will never rest.

Salma does not ask for them and there is one dream that she cannot forget.

She is lying in her bed and the dead come through the windows and through the door. They fill the room till they cannot move and they stare down at her as she tries to rest. She can hear them in the house, outside, in the village, an endless street party of the dead.

She asks them to leave and it takes them a while to clear. The last one turns to her and says, 'We mean you no trouble, we mean you no distress. We come to you because you are open, you do not forget us and how else can we live on except in someone's head?'

THE THOUSAND NIGHTS

When the killers come in, the buckets are already prepared. She has lined them up against the wall and each person takes one and begins to clean. They are neat even if there is a lot of blood. By the time they've finished, no sign remains of what they have done.

One night, the eldest sits and Salma braids her hair. She scolds the killer for her messiness, she reminds her there is more to life than guns and politics, that there is a soul, that there will be an end and each person will be made to answer for their deeds.

The killer nods and the others feed and in the weeks ahead, there will be another night like this with the buckets lined up so they can go home and their families will remain innocent of how their children spend their time.

She once considered casting them off, telling them to find another house, but she can't think of an alternative that won't compromise their safety.

They are younger, children to her, and most of all she wants to protect them from the world.

Three of them she will bury, one will die on the concrete and no amount of water will clear the blood from the floor. She imagines she can still see it the next morning, but even on her hands and knees, eye to the ground, the ground is clean and there is no sign of what happened the night before.

The killer.

My braided killer.

The one I will bury again and again in my nights in the years to come.

The one I cannot abandon, whose soul I tried to protect even in death, the one I will not shoo from my dreams no matter how much it causes me distress.

She sees the killer, she sees that face and she ties the end of the braid again and again for a thousand nights.

THE END

Salma woke wondering where the time had gone. Once she had been in school and it had been peaceful and provided a rhythm for her years but that time was long ago and now there was little to distinguish one year from the next.

She marked her years by events in her family. There was the year Alaa went overseas, there was the year Aliyah came to visit with her husband and kids. She had been glad to see Aliyah but it made her think *I should have gone overseas when I had the chance.*

Aliyah spoke of wonders, she spoke of organisation that would never be known here, not in a million years. *The generosity of the place is special while here ...*

She did not have to add anything else for them to understand.

Salma noticed details as Aliyah noticed them and she could not expel them from her mind.

A machine for clothes, another for dishes, people who had enough time to cut lawns. Free education from childhood into the adult years. Free hospitals, doctors who smiled, a place where no one collapsed on the street.

When she imagined her own end, Salma saw herself collapsing publicly. No one helped her and they walked over or around her. Meanwhile Aliyah—may God protect her—lay in a bed, tended by doctors and nurses, her children and husband and everyone else smiling as she slipped into the next life.

She shook these thoughts because comparison was a child of envy and Salma had been taught to guard her heart against this.

When Aliyah left, Salma had been relieved and she realised she was happier for her sister to be away than present here where she would be reminded always of another life.

Sometimes she dreams it. The end is a wave and it crashes on her head and from it there is no escape. One time there was a slip in this dream. Aliyah was next to her and Salma was swept away as the wave broke. Aliyah was left standing, smiling and untouched.

SLEEPLESS

Days she is wakeful, through the nights too, and she moves through the world with her eyes open but she lives as if in a dream.

Her family says *you need to get some sleep.*

She agrees but this does not help her with the mechanics of sleep.

Alert in the night, the fog of the day, and she has little accidents in the hours she is awake.

She is out, far at sea, with no way home.

On edge, *I can do this no more.*

THE DAZE

The day Salma almost died began like the others of her life. She had her breakfast, she dressed, she brushed her hair, she strapped her feet into her shoes and she was off to begin her day.

Salma had listened to her mother and made a list because *that will stop you from buying what you don't need*. Never mind she only had money for a few essentials on her list.

On the journey in, she made a note of the three things she could not return home without or else that night there wouldn't be enough to eat.

She blamed herself because lately she had been distracted, lately she could not focus, lately she noticed a special trouble in her head. She shook her head rapidly, she blinked, but the world may as well have been a blur.

Her teachers once said she was stupid and she heard her neighbours whispering *I hear that Salma is actually dumb*, and there might have been some truth to this but the trouble with her head was something else. She'd stare at the prices but not take the numbers in, she'd stare at lists but the letters might as well have been written by another's hand. Her mother would repeat her name to get her attention and even then they knew, as Salma did, that her response was very slow.

They thought her slowness was deliberate, that it was an act she was putting on.

Still the daze was something else.

In her last years, she had heard stories of people in rooms where bombs had gone off.

I could not hear, I could not see, there were weeks where I was always on edge.

I never recovered. I am lost there still. I am no longer the person I consider to be my real self.

Except they had a bomb and she did not, or she had a bomb but it was on the news or in the city far away. And on the day she almost died, she walked into the path of a car. It slammed its brakes and hit a pole and in her daze she realised she'd almost become one of those dolls in the safety test videos.

She mumbled an apology and the driver was outraged at her indifference but there wasn't much she could do so she continued on.

Her list had ten items, she could only afford three, it would be better if she held the bar low and tried not to forget the bread.

Her mother berates her for only bringing home the bread. Her mother is slumped in the corner and they both know it but don't say it, that Jamal is likely dead and there are rumours that the dirt beside the well looks very fresh.

She tells her mother about the car that almost hit her and she makes the mistake of comparing the experience to a bomb, that in recent months she feels she has misplaced her spirit and she may as well have misplaced her head.

Her mother says she is disrespecting the dead and the seriously ill who are not right in the mind. Her mother says she should not compare herself to those worse off than her.

We are in a war and people are dying and that is not the same as forgetting and only bringing home the bread.

Salma falls silent and that night she sees the car and it almost hits her but the details are fading which is a mercy and already she is distracted by the day that lies ahead.

THE SIGN

Salma meant to marry him even though Ahmed insisted he had been altered by the war. 'The person I was before is not who I am now and there is no reversing time's hand.'

She told him she loved him, she told him it was meant to be, but sometimes she noticed Ahmed staring into space and she knew he did not always have this habit. She asked him about this space and what he saw. He shrugged and held out his hand for hers. 'I am somewhere else but that is all I can tell you about this place where my mind is.'

Though the war was done (or was it?), Salma felt its presence in the air. It was on the news every day, it had a long aftermath and no one dared used the word *peace* just yet. She saw signs of it in the buildings, she saw it in the hesitation of people to begin their lives properly again. More talk about going overseas and there was a belief that what had been broken could not be fixed but at least one could escape for another chance abroad.

Ahmed said the right things and for a while Salma believed them in love but when he formally asked for her hand, she went for a walk and stared into the ocean for a long time. Today was green and the sun was happy. She should have also been happy but she was not.

She saw the ocean and she could not see the emptiness Ahmed talked about.

She saw the clouds and how they hovered over the water, each set unique and nothing like the days before.

She saw the birds and they were alive and spun with energy in the sky.

She saw this space and saw life and she asked God for a sign that to marry him was right. Any sign would have sufficed. A dream, a tree, the sun shining the right way, but God was silent on the matter, so when Ahmed returned for her answer, she told him the truth.

He stared into space again and said he understood and she believed him, and each went separately to whatever was to be their fate.

HOPE

Salma had once been hopeful of recovery. She would recover her spirits, Ahmed would return, the dead would be brought back to life, what was lost would be found, and once again her hope would be alive.

At some point in the eighties or nineties, she put down the parcel, lost it and then it was never found again.

The war had ended . . . peace at last . . . the dead were immobilised in the ground. The only time they became animated was in the night-time, but even she admitted she could no longer keep them in her heart.

There was the return to elections and this was a promising sign, but all sides (and there were many) quietly muttered about the side that deserved the most blame.

Ahmed was wounded—not in his neck, leg or head, but in his spirit—and though he still smiled, he was no longer the man she had promised forever to love.

And her family, once they had lived together, but now they were children of the world. Phone calls, money, presents, none of which was a person, and each person went to the life that destiny prescribed.

Even she was not the same and it was not the hand of time or how she was now bent when once she had stood ever so straight. No, the change in her was different.

Once there had been promise and now she was grateful for the pittance the universe continued to provide.

THE SELLOUT

Salma faced her niece and began . . .

'Once upon a time, I cared about the war. I cared about politics. I cared about the future of the world. These things were around us and you could not avoid them. Decades of this and it becomes part of your system, it becomes part of what you breathe, but you get to a time, maybe it has to do with age, and you don't have energy anymore for the anger required for the injustices of the world. Once you would have screamed at the TV, you would have thrown a shoe, you would have stopped being friends with people who had different politics to you. You would have protested, you would have shouted in the street, and I did all those things for many years, and then sometime—it was in my thirties—I realised I felt tired easily, that my life had other things and that I needed my energy for them, for the people in my life, that me caring about the President's words meant the garden wouldn't be looked after, that the vegetables I needed in the kitchen did not grow so well because my energy was spent elsewhere, that this anger left me empty, and my preference was to be able to function in my every day, and from there it was easy, I gave it up, I stayed out of conversations and the million other times people asked me to care. I still did care, I really did, but I had no more energy for it and I refused to react as I had once done on demand when they asked. I had had enough. In a sense you could say I walked away and there are people who say I'm a sellout, and maybe that is the case, but I am happy again and I can see the light is greater than the dark.'

The niece absorbed the words and wondered what it changed in her own life. She imagined herself lying in bed, her aunt's words reverberating in her head, being moved to epiphanies, beginning her day with a spark.

She told her father about the conversation and he rolled his eyes. 'The only part that's right is that Salma is a sellout and this is evidence she has her head in the clouds. She is lost to the cause and worse, she is a lost cause, and my advice to you is to make sure you keep away.'

1973

The recovery—when she thought of recovery—would return her to the past, specifically to 1973. The fighting was underway because someone had pressed play, but the bloodiest was yet to come and she still suffered from the belief that given time it would pass, and what was before would come back again, and they would move freely, untraumatised by the world.

1973 was the pinnacle but when the war closed out, numbness set in and Salma struggled to remember the years before. No more did anyone speak of sitting out the year, no more did anyone say *it is like a tropical storm we have to endure, and there have been storms plenty that have passed over us before.*

That sense was eradicated by the blood of 1974.

There was too much blood under the bridge and no one could believe that with time the river's water could be made clean once again.

The mood was that they were in it for the long haul and realising there was the possibility that they wouldn't make it through.

It was not just the bodies surfacing and that the dead were family and friends.

It was not just the leaders calling for retaliation to the retaliation to pay back their retaliation which was for our your my retaliation without an end in sight.

It was not just that no one talked of the future anymore. It was as if next year, next month, next week would not happen and they were restricted to the possibilities contained in the pitiful state they were allowed on this day.

It was not just that she had plans once and now she found it difficult to make it to the bedroom door.

It was not just that she was meant to turn twenty in 1973 and her life was meant to properly begin. The day had passed unnoticed and there was enough blame going around already that she did not also want to blame them for forgetting it was her birthday.

In the end, there should have been a cake but there was not, there should have been a beginning but it felt like she was living the days of the end and what really changed was her sense. Once she had hope, a smile, she had straight shoulders and a plan. Now she sought out a refuge, a quiet place, and from there on, Salma counted it as the year she started withdrawing from the world.

FAILURES

They had failed and Salma knew it was not her fault.

Take her education, for example. She had done one year of university and then the war started and later life got in the way of her going back. She had meant to but it was too expensive, not essential, and she was busy trying to keep herself afloat.

There were people who said they would return and they did, and she envied these people their will, but their energies were outside her range on a day by day.

Or the question of marriage. Ahmed was traumatised and she had tried loving him but he was not the person he once was, and it was a fact beyond her and his control. They had discussed it but this bucket was endless and it was a problem that could not be solved.

Or the people who left. Some returned. Some did not. And this was not counting the ones premature in the ground.

Numbers, numbers always going up without an end and the sensible thing to do was to stop trying to control life with the old stranglehold.

And counting was what Salma did and this was what Salma considered as her failure in the night.

THE LIGHTS

She is never again the same. She can never go back. The tide of life has moved and it exists beyond her reach.

This is not pessimism. Four decades of hoping and she admits her efforts—judge them as you wish—have failed.

There was a war. It broke over them. They never found their way back to the before and they did not find whatever it was they each privately wished for.

Salma counts the impact but the list is great and the list leads nowhere near the light she needs and so she abandons it.

What conclusion is there for her regarding these events that are the territory of historians? She descends through the years till night-time claims her and then she begins to dream.

Some days she wakes from blankness.

Some days she wakes and she knows people have died in the night.

Some days she wakes and she has dreamed but she cannot pinpoint a single image, a single scene.

She wants to ask the people around her if they have recovered, she wants to establish if it is only her, but she is conscious of digging at wounds that others are trying to close.

And this is where Salma finds herself. Her life has momentum but no direction, she has events that she cannot work into a pattern. Instead she has this place of dark matter. Life is ticking but someone has forgotten to turn the lights back on.

ROLLING DOWN THE HILL

There is this hill that Salma used to roll down when she was younger. It was close to her house and it was the hill that the kids used to hang around. From it, she could see the sky and the clouds hanging over the sea, and when she thinks of the hill now, it seems the greenest place she has ever seen, especially against the colour of the sea behind.

It was Amal who first suggested they roll down the hill. It was always her daring them to try new things, but she would later grow out of this habit as one outgrows clothes that used to fit. Amal stood at the top and pointed to the bottom and instructed them in the art of rolling down the hill.

Salma remembers the sensation, how the grass concealed the many bumps. At first her thoughts spun and then her mind became quiet and she wanted to call out but she could not put the words together.

At the bottom, they dusted each other off and removed grass from each other's hair. Amal would shove grass in their faces but she stopped after Lubna snuck a handful down the back of her dress. Amal got so itchy and they all laughed at the look on her face.

Salma does the calculation and it has been fifty years at least and the hill is not what it once was. There is rubbish, it is where the kids go to smoke and she cannot trust what the grass hides underneath. Still it would be nice to roll again, to remember the sensation from long ago. Over the days, she begins to clean the hill, putting the rubbish into bags that she burns out the back of the house. The young ones see her doing this and they help her and again it becomes the hill from her childhood that has now long ago passed.

She becomes a fixture on this hill and she watches as the young ones take up the tradition of rolling. They laugh and scream and chase each other round with threatening handfuls of grass.

On the day she is dared to roll down the hill, Salma does not need to be told twice.

She presses her skirt between her knees and once upon a time she was silent but now all she can do is laugh.

THE FLAMES OF PEACE

First it was the cart, then it was the permit and now it is where he stands. He moves the cart to another area and still they follow him. *You cannot be here. If you do not move, we will arrest you.*

It does not matter how much he argues, it does not matter how much he points to the stands and carts around him. *They do the same as me. Why don't you chase them too?*

He speaks but he may as well be silent because they do not hear him. Their eyes rest a fraction above his head and he worries what will happen if he disappears. His mother, his sisters, his uncle, what will be left for them except to beg on the streets? He sees another future where he is not chased from where he is set up so they can breakfast on something other than bread and fruit. Each morning, his mother kisses him before he leaves. 'Without you, what would we do?' His sister helps him load the cart before she leaves for university. One day she will finish her studies, one day there will be more money, but his lot in the meantime is to evade them street to street, stuck in the knowledge that there is nothing else he can do.

They arrest him, they kick his cart to the side and they laugh at what his scales will fetch on the street. Their sole value is his livelihood. Anyone else would throw them in the bin.

If I do not sell, I do not eat and my family is out on the streets. If I sell, you cast me here and demand papers that do not exist. You have made me this target but everyone else is left in peace. Yesterday it was the cart and permit, today it is where I stand. Tell me, why am I denied what is allowed every other human being?

There is no answer. They talk among themselves and he has ceased to exist. He has no cart, he has no scales, he is left without a thing to offer the world.

It is fine, it is fine, I am allowed the peace of the other world.

He takes the petrol and sets himself alight. They scream for him to stop, they try to put out the flames.

You have not allowed me the life of a dog but you cannot deny me this.

TAXI

When my father was younger, he said he would learn English. *It is the language of the world, it is the future here.*

He took us out of our school and enrolled us in another. Arabic, English, a little bit of French. We will be citizens of the world.

How was he to learn English as an adult man? There were no courses in the village, he could not read at a level to enter university. His one choice was to read over our shoulders and for us to teach him the words. He put a satellite dish on the roof and we only ever watched English shows night and day. He had the TV tuned to children's shows because they spoke slowly and he could understand.

Sometimes I heard him saying over and over the words he had learned that day. If he forgot them, he would take out the paper from his pocket and memorise them again.

He drove his taxi to town each day and tried to find tourists who could help him practise his new words. Most of the time he found locals who spoke Arabic and once knew French, but they remembered little from disuse. Their loss, they said, was a lesson to him. *If you wish to learn a language, use it every day or it is gone.*

I used to imagine these people he met and wonder how he asked them if they knew English. *Hello, where are you going, do you know English words?*

So many days he returned and he practised his English on us. When we got older, we asked him for a separate TV so we could watch the shows the kids spoke about at school. We left him our books and he continued to practise on his own. *One day the travellers will come and I will be able to speak to them in their tongue.*

We grew up and we left to have families of our own. When we visited, he would try his words on us but we asked him to please stop. We had forgotten much of what we had once known. *We said to him one day our children will go to school and you can practise with them. You will be older and you won't need the taxi and TV as much.*

He did not listen and even though there were no travellers, he left in his taxi at dawn and he did not return until very late. We asked him about travellers and what words he had learned but he ignored us more and more. He would sit in the taxi and when we spoke to him through the window, he pretended he did not understand a single thing.

My mother told us he listened to English radio and only left the car to eat. *He does not listen, he does not speak, he does not sleep in the bed.*

We waited for him to leave the taxi and called someone we knew and sold the taxi off. We gave my father the money but he ripped it up and said something we could not understand.

Day and night now, he does not leave the house. He listens to the radio, he watches the TV, he reads our books and writes out new words he has learned. He teaches the young ones and speaks to them daily. Everyone else, he shakes his head and says he does not understand.

THE BEGGAR

Years ago there appeared at the foot of the building a begging man. His trousers were grey and he seemed to be missing a leg. These beggars were good at appearing to suffer a misfortune. His hand was out and his eyes were turned blind to the sky.

In the morning and in the evening I would see him on my way to work. Others gave him money but I stepped around him and ignored his false eyes. Each day there was a plea. 'Sir, I need some change.'

Just as this building has its beggar so do others in the area. It is as if they work in agreement, dividing who has each building so that they do not crowd in, competing for the same few coins. One woman sat with her child, each holding out their hands. The child's clothes were dirty and the woman always had tears in her eyes. There was a pair who twitched as if possessed, spitting at people's legs as they went past. This made people avoid them and if they were at that building, I always crossed the street.

The truth is man is guaranteed death, taxes and beggars in the street. I am grateful for the guard at the door and how only a resident is allowed in. Buildings without a guard end up with families moving in to live beneath the stairs. Once they are in, it is impossible to be rid of them again.

The one outside our door was there six or eight years. On this point, everyone in our building disagrees. The guard says it was longer, closer to ten. If it was six years or ten, we would have seen him thousands of times, more than I have seen members of my family.

We speak of him now because he is gone. Is he dead or has he moved on? They talk about a search or raising money. For what, who knows, but anyhow we don't have a name. This talk goes through the building one day but we can't even agree on when he disappeared.

Plans are made, plans are thrown out, and then we discover a new beggar has moved in. He has crutches and his broken feet are stretched out before him. He cannot walk, his sign says, and plans are discussed for helping him. He will be given money, he will be made to stand, he will be cared for as family.

That night, each returns to their apartment and the guard locks out the world outside.

The next morning, I study the new one. I nod at him but his eyes never lift to my face. I think of the coins in my pocket and continue on my way.

THE MOUNTAIN

When he made his first billion, Sami bought the top half of the mountain. Once his grandparents had lived at its foot but now he would have a view to the sea and the mountains beyond.

His first point of business was the road. Bulldozers, excavators, trucks and workers battled a road to the top. They layered the gravel and sprayed the asphalt and he thought *I can now build my house.*

He flew in an architect, he flew in consultants recommended by his friends. The design would be Mediterranean: white walls, orange tiles, a palace as a backdrop to his life.

The first night he spent in his palace, he lit up every light. He imagined the people below looking upwards. Yes, the mountain has a king at its top. His sole regret was that he could not be in two places at once: to see the mountain being lit for the first time while being the one to flick the switch. Sami would ask tomorrow and his people would give him a detailed report.

He thought to live at the top.

He thought his apartment in the city would be sold.

He had not yet walked through his home when his guard called him. 'There is a line of beggars at the door.'

It was not enough to own the mountain and the road to its top. Both needed to be fenced off.

He called the builders and said, 'Tomorrow you will build me a fence.'

The fence took them sixty days and at each gate there were guards. One day he was being driven home and he looked up into the night. *There is my home. Who knew a mountain could be owned?* He noticed then the beggars lining both sides of the public road. He would soon pass his fence and these people would be left behind.

He wondered about the poverty in the world, the people who lived on the streets with their hands held out. The beggars visited him in his dreams and for days they bothered him more than he cared to admit.

Sami considered his options. He could build another fence. He could sit nightly in his palace with the lights turned off. A helicopter could drop him off so he could access his palace without their sight greeting him every day.

He remembered his apartment in the city, how he could come and go as he pleased. No one knew him from the others on the street and the traffic hid his presence better than any mountaintop.

What could he do with half a mountain in a country where he was the richest man? He divided up the land and sold it off. Houses were built that were smaller replicas of his own. The number of cars going and coming made the turns dangerous and the beggars abandoned the road for the city again. He slept in the apartment, dreaming of the mountaintop.

Tomorrow he would go, tomorrow he would drive to the top. He would enjoy the view, he would study the land he owned.

Leave these thoughts for tomorrow.

So he slept, hoping for peace in the valley and peace at the top.

SILENCE

There was the snake. That was the first sign. It had been nailed to the door while she was out the back. Most people would have heeded this warning but she insisted this was her home. She took the snake down, buried it near the well and wiped the door so that no blood remained.

Next there was the car. They deflated the tyres and scratched the body with their keys. This did not matter so much because it was rusting anyway. The business with the tyres was something else. She had no pump and there was no one who would lend her one so she used her bicycle more and made sure to lock it up every night. As she rode through town, they laughed and called out their jokes.

The third time they broke in she was out for groceries. The furniture was overturned and they had destroyed what they could. The toaster and microwave were smashed on the floor and the power cords to the washing machine and fridge had been cut.

She stood holding her bicycle, surveying her place. She had food and the cups and plates could still be used. She raised the phone to call for repairs but it had been cut at the wall as well.

They came for her in the middle of the night and made her strip to her underclothes. They paraded her in the town square, kicking her when she slowed her pace. In the morning, a stranger took pity on her and found her some clothes. She was given tea and a bun and she considered then her life. She would leave with what she needed, she would carry her valuables secured to her back.

When she told this story later, people cut her off. *It is your fault entirely*, they said, *for not registering the attacks on your life early on.*

She argued initially as she had argued when they urged her to leave but when she realised she could not win, she left her story and favoured silence once again.

BENEATH THE SHADE OF MEMORY

Amir is young. He cannot pinpoint the age but he might have been five or six. He runs to his grandmother and he sits in her lap. She covers his eyes, she tickles him, she laughs and laughs. She chops up lettuce and feeds him the crunchy bits. She halves the tomato and adds salt to the piece she offers him. When the salad is made, she sets out a bowl and together they eat.

He remembers her pointing out the tree which is not as tall as him. 'One day, this tree will be so large it will cover everything here with shade. I love this tree but do you know who I love more than this tree?'

'Who?'

'You know who I love but this is a secret only kept for you.'

He is older. He works with his grandfather in the field. The ground is ploughed then planted for the new season. For their lunch, they have bread, olives and cheese. After they have eaten, his grandfather produces an orange from his basket and this they eat before returning to the field.

His grandfather speaks to him from where he works. 'One day when we are gone, this land will belong to you.'

He thinks of the tree his grandmother loves and how it already covers the house. She is shaded by it daily and beneath it is her favourite spot in the afternoon. They are so old to him and one day they will be older still and he hopes that they will sit together in the evening and tell him stories about their lives as they sometimes do. His father comes to collect him and Amir smiles at them sitting beneath the tree as he is led away.

When he marries, he insists the wedding start at their house. There he is shaved and his grandparents watch on. Later they will take the car arranged once he goes to collect his bride.

He always remembers that day and how his grandmother, who has trouble breathing, stood up and began to dance. He tells himself one day he will visit them with his bride.

He visits often but he visits alone. When the troubles start, he makes excuses, *she is busy with her work*. His grandmother clears a spot next to her and says, 'Do you remember when you were this high?' She holds out her hand in front of her to indicate how tall he had been at the age of five.

In the first days when it falls apart, he comes to stay in their house. The tree's shade is complete and one can forget that these are days of summer and that each day promises heat without relief. They speak as in the old days but there is no work to occupy them.

His father finds him there. 'Don't you think it would be better to be at home where you might sort out this business with your wife?'

The first time this happens, he argues and defends his place. He has visited all her relations but not once has she come to visit his grandparents with him. 'If I had known she would be like this, I wouldn't have married her at all.'

His grandfather tells him to calm down. His grandmother tells him not to yell.

His father leaves and he is alone with them once more. He wonders what the future holds for them all but then his grandmother takes his hand and pats it and he could have been a boy once more.

'This tree,' she says, 'has been here since you were small and it will be here after we are all gone. Do not forget this will one day be yours and this will always be your home.'

He thinks of the apartment and how he cannot wait to walk out the door every day, and what carries him is not a memory but the knowledge that there is this tree and beneath it are his grandparents and one day he will have the peace that he counts as theirs alone.

SERVICES AT HOME

Um Talal hired Jamal because he was strong. She was older and she could not reach the trees and it tired her to maintain the house as in the days of old. She asked around and was told about Jamal. 'If you come for a trial, we will see what can be arranged.'

He said he would arrive at eight and he was as good as his word. She had not forgotten the other trials that failed. One had turned up two hours late, the other never showed his face, but Jamal worked and he did not rest until it was time for lunch.

The raking of leaves, the cutting of trees, he dug the garden beds as well. He collected the groceries from the car, and she could trust him to buy what was on the list and give her the correct change. She dared not speak too much of his honesty for fear that someone else would entice him away with a better pay.

Sometimes she made a meal and if he had not eaten yet, she would invite him to sit in the courtyard inside. She knew if people knew, they would speak and she would never be free of the gossip and lies. Still, it would be silly not to invite him to share her meal when there was more than enough for two.

Salma was the first to tell her what the neighbours had said. 'You should not be having meals together in your place. You know better than to do this because of how they talk.'

She argued, she pointed out nothing was going on and God was her witness in any case.

Salma dismissed this. 'God may be your witness but people are tried by other people.'

If they were so stupid as to make up lies and rumours, she might as well continue eating with Jamal. This was interpreted as provocation. This handyman not only did jobs around the house but also shared her bed.

Now everyone came around to remind her of her place. 'You are an old woman, you have children his age. Think of your reputation and what people will say when you go between them.'

She shrugged and went about her day.

When she called her friends, they said they had plans. Only Salma said the truth. 'If you continue like this, we can't be friends. You may not care but I have to live among them and I will be made to hear the words they say.'

She knew what this meant, she knew she was left with a choice. She called Jamal in and said, 'I am sorry. I have no need for your services anymore.'

THE OTHER WOMAN

When he brought Amna home, they told her to throw rice. She looked at the handful and let it drop on the floor.

Everything will be the same, sweetie, believe me, nothing will change.

He came to visit her bed and she barricaded the door.

I am tired. I wish to be left alone.

Later he said to her, 'What about my rights as a man?'

To this, she packed up his things. One, two, three, and she threw them out the door.

He came to prefer the other one and this he made no effort to hide.

They told her about sweetness, politeness, the benefits of ha ha ha.

She pointed to the door and said, 'I would like you to leave this house.'

Finally she was implored to remember God, religion and what was deemed to be the law.

She slammed the door at their backs and shouted, 'Your God, your laws. They will never be mine.'

THE GHOSTS OF WAR

The war is over and the soldiers are heading home. Once a school stood there and that building has lost its face. Even the shacks on the beach have been dismantled to prevent shady deals on the sand.

His mother is waiting and she runs up, kissing him on both cheeks. 'I started to believe you would never come home.'

His aunt stands beside his mother. Three sons, two daughters, and no one knows if they are in a grave or if they have met another fate unknown. She kisses him also and when she wipes the tears from her eyes, more appear in their place.

They walk home with him as one would with a child. He reaches often for his mother's hand and notices her skin is not as smooth as it once was. His aunt and mother chat to each other and no one seems to care that he does not contribute a word.

He has visited over the years but it was always in haste. The break of a day, leaving as quickly as he arrived. This is the first time he can finally look around and survey his home.

Around the back there once were orange and lemon trees, but now it is full of tents. He counts nine. 'Each one is a family's,' his aunt says. 'They will move on but it will take time and anyhow it gets rid of the silence around the house.' The bedroom out the back has been turned to storage and he is told he will be given the room out the front. 'It will be comfortable. You will have that space to yourself.'

He remembers his four brothers and his sister and how they used to sleep side by side. In the summer, they opened the windows and tried counting the stars in the night sky. Fatin would tell them to sleep which made them talk even louder than before. Finally a kick and there would be silence before they laughed and talked once more.

He watches his mother praying and he remembers a time when they prayed all in a row. Two ducks and their ducklings and now his mother prays alone. His father is buried beyond the tents and each day she goes to his grave. Only one lies at her feet but this is where she remembers all of them. His aunt joins her and then they return to make their lunch. He thinks of their silent words, quietness offered to the sky, and whether these prayers are ever heard. He asks his mother if she believes her calls ever reach their mark.

She studies him for a long time as his aunt watches on and he knows they are thinking of those who are gone. Finally she says, 'Perhaps they do, perhaps they don't, but this is how I keep them alive on this Earth.'

That night, he dreams of them, the ghosts who never made it home. They walk past him one by one and then they fade into the dark. They continue to visit him nightly and he hears them speaking in the day. He sees Fatin on the swings, he sees his brothers climbing trees that no longer exist. His aunt's children chase each other round and round as they did when they were ten. Everywhere he carries them and he doesn't get out of bed because they will not leave him alone.

One time, his aunt finds him sleeping in the height of the day. He is sweating and his cousins fill his entire eye.

She dresses him, ties his shoes and urges him to stand. Together they walk to his father's grave and she begins to pray but not silently as she does every other time. She calls for mercy, she calls for them to be kept safe. An hour and she recites the verses she knows. He can hear nothing but her voice and finally his family recede one by one. When she finishes, the two of them are standing alone.

'The dead are not alive. They belong in the ground. If you remember them, they will be at peace and your heart will be left free for your days.'

The next day he goes with his mother and aunt, and the three of them stare at the ground. He cannot remember the words he says or the verse on his tongue but for once he forgets the recent years. He eats his food, and makes an effort to sweep the floor. He sits with coffee in the sun and he even laughs. He is alive but by visiting them, they are not forgotten and stay at bay.

DISTURBANCE AND THEN A DREAM

Omar remembers that night, he remembers it as if it were a dream. There is the film, there is gunfire, there are all his friends. He will never be rid of this memory but sometimes remembering them is the only way he can sleep.

The evening started with them watching a film. American, dubbed recently, they were excited by the director's latest offering.

The hero was reloading his rifle when Omar heard a crash. The others did not notice. Perhaps the crash was in the film. He said nothing, simply continued with his tea.

The next crash and they jumped out of their seats. This was close by, it was their street, and no, it was not the film. One went to the roof, one to the window, they killed the lights and switched off the TV.

Another crash, closer. Someone shouted, 'We need to get out of here.'

They ran to the back and the last one shut the door. They need not have bothered because they heard the breaking of the front door.

Later, he will learn the details, he will have time to pad the memory.

The camp had been sealed off and it did not matter if they ran or walked. They were lined up in rows against a wall that had been there their entire life. When they wheeled over the machine gun, Omar thought *this is like bringing speakers to the party.*

He does not watch, he shuts his eyes as he does later in his memory. The bodies will lie there, they will be facedown in their shirts and jeans. The shake of a shoulder will not disturb the flies that have settled in. The streets will be photographed, the videos will capture everything.

In his mind, he traces their bodies, an invisible banner linking their memory.

Bashir, Bassam, Ahmed, Abdul, Mustapha, Kamel, Jalaleddine.

He opens his eyes in the darkness once his recital is complete. They trouble his sleep so much and he wonders how the guilty ever sleep.

THE BULLY: PART II

Come now   let us talk   let us not pretend   lies and truth they are sounds   no more   a word offered   passed man to man you speak truth   this you say   please do not misunderstand it is destiny   yes indeed   they will be misconstrued   the dead are protected   theirs is the final word   me I am condemned my actions tried   my character judged   believe me   I meant not what I said   I have been taken out of context   they deify him   demonise me   they set us apart   he is light   I am cast as night   we play out a battle   the masses cry   they weep one long moan   this I deplore   tell me friend   my silent one you watcher of the sides   I am guilty   I am a wrath   what does that make you   watchful friend   the stander-by   walk on now   the sums and we a part   nothing more   I cannot stay   I have duties   bills papers a life   to them I must attend   history judges   the audience is silent   their faces masked   they are never named   if I am the arm   you are the back   your silence is compliance   but but but   we all protest the mirror brought to our face   but nothing   call me bully little watcher   veiled unnamed   you are my favourite friend.

THE PARTS THEY PLAY

The war broke out and she decided to call her dad. Weeks and weeks they do not speak and the weeks become months and then they are so many years. She imagines herself starting this story. She imagines how later she will tell this story to someone else. *We hadn't spoken for years but then the war broke out* . . . because a war can heal a rift and there is no need for other details to add to her case. She imagines the scenarios: he won't answer, he will ignore her call, he will answer and she'll hear his smile, he will answer and he'll be gruff. All the scenarios are happening as she listens to the ring.

They once argued and it was always politics. Their meetings would begin with attempts at lightness and end in a stall. Once they agreed and now they don't but is that a reason not to speak?

She remembers the last time they met. She brought vegetables, she made tea, he refused to leave the TV. *Why do you make me choose between you and the TV? Why can't you just sit with me?*

She did sit, in fact, to prove that she could. After watching him watching the screen, she left and never returned.

He wrote her a note and she remembers him once saying *it is too late for anything else.*

I have decided to leave this world.

But how and why? It is against our religion. You're the one who taught me this.

I am tired of the repetition in this life. You have hope and it is not justified.

Without hope, there is only despair. These are your lines.

I hoped you would return but we all have our pride.

She has no response. Nothing, the lines don't form.

That is not a reason but as there is conflict abroad, there is conflict at home. This is not your fault. Sometimes our only choice is the choice not to take part.

She doesn't take part, he doesn't take part, they don't take part, she doesn't take part, he doesn't take part, they don't take part, she doesn't, he doesn't, they don't, she, he, they . . .

She sees him: a single figure, the wave grows large, the war breaks out, the TV blacks out and she makes her call.

She thinks to follow him so they can argue this properly once and for all. Once she argued with him and now she argues with herself. He said, she said, they said, round and round we go, but as long as there is an argument, there she will make her stand.

THE GOLDEN LIRA

Hassan Effendi was a man born in the twilight of the Ottoman Empire. His grandchildren remembered the way he dressed and the way he spoke. He wore broad pants held up by a cloth belt woven around his middle and he was never seen without his fez. His speech was filled with Turkish words that they asked him to explain. Between them, they agreed he should stick to one language if he wished to be understood.

They remembered him always with the walking stick. Forever in their memories, he is propped up by the stick. His clothes, his words and his stick, they were what made Hassan Effendi distinct. It did not matter to him that Turkish and then French had faded from their land and now children learned English instead. The TV said Mandarin would be next but when they tried to draw him into a debate about language he said, 'But Turkish is how I think,' and then he told them he needed silence and they knew to be quiet from the day they were born. Break the silence and earn a whack across the knees. The stick felt like metal rather than wood and their parents drew them away and said, 'Leave Hassan Effendi. He needs his rest.'

They used to play a game to guess his age. To their children's eyes, he was one hundred or two and their speculation even reached three, but once they became adults themselves, they studied the photos and thought he couldn't have been more than eighty. When they floated their revised numbers with their parents, they displayed the certificate of his death. It was stamped, it was official and the papers had his death at ninety-two.

They joked about him often and if they had not all known him and been able to verify the facts, they would have doubted their memories were real. His black pants—he only had two pairs—the fez for his head and the walking stick he left behind.

Once they had dared to suggest he modernise. *Some new clothes, drop those old-fashioned words, surgery so you're not so reliant on that walking stick.*

He whacked at them but they laughed and howled and refused to move from his side. 'The way I live is the way I think and not even fifty of you will make me change.'

At that time, Hassan Effendi had ten grandchildren and later even the chorus of a larger group would not make him change his mind.

When he died, they found he had a golden coin hidden in his shirt. It was pure gold, a lira, currency from Ottoman times. The story went that when he was younger, Hassan Effendi had put a year's work into that coin and it was his security in the world. 'It does not matter what empires rise and which ones fall, I still have this coin and so long as I have this coin, I can stay as I am.'

They were all adults by then and they doubted the story because they had not heard it from his mouth. It had the sound of a myth about an ancestor long gone, and besides, if he valued it so much, he would have spoken of the coin when he was alive. This was their reasoning so they went ahead and had the coin melted down. They split the value evenly and did not speak of their nightmares where Hassan Effendi called their actions a crime. These were just dreams, like wasps that were repelled when ignored, but when it came to his clothes and the walking stick, they placed them carefully into a chest and reminded each other where they lay.

They reminisced as we all do when we have the time. They took their children into their arms and told them about Hassan Effendi. *He is your ancestor, he has faded much like an empire, much like a dream.* The children would laugh and joke and Hassan Effendi's belongings would be brought out as proof. They tried on the hat, they took turns with the pants. They all practised walking with the stick and they laughed as they whacked each other. It did not matter. These were made-up stories about an ancestor in a dream. Put away the clothes, put away the stick, at the end of their reminiscing, he would cease to exist.

HUMAN SHIELDS

It is an average wall. It is forgettable and you have walked past it a thousand times. It is brick, you think, but you're not sure if it is grey or the dullest white. Every day this does not matter but you want the details right so you can write the story. Get the details right and the story becomes fact, and what you're after is not the land of story but the world of fact. Numbers, details, dates and times, persons involved, a date of birth, height, weight, precise coordinates of the place.

The wall is thirty years old. It was once white and time has faded it to grey. Twenty-three metres high, it was once the fence around an apartment block. Or perhaps it was the building's side. Never mind, it is thirty years old. It was built by Abdul Hanif and his sons. You do not know Abdul Hanif or his sons, if they are two or three, but the detail adds weight to the delivery and it gives the story a foundation that is concrete and strong.

When the child is shot, she is twelve years, one month and a single day. She shelters at her mother's side who is calling out for help. It is crossfire and they will argue over whose bullet it is. In fact, today there is doubt cast over the existence of the little girl but Rayan is her name and she is only twelve at the time. They leave their house, they walk past the wall you and I know, they hide at its side as gunfire breaks out. It is okay, the gunfire has nothing to do with them, it is not intended for this woman and her girl.

Later—it is always later—it will be said that they did not know the mother and Rayan were caught against the wall. In this time, someone—a foreigner, a local, on our side or against—will have captured those moments and shared them with the world. There is the world, there is the mother (Fatin bint Abu Salim), there is Rayan pressed against Fatin's legs. The girl has her eyes shut but her mother stares at the world eyes open wide. She has her arm around her daughter; it is in the photo you have studied thousands of times. You wonder about their stupidity, you wonder why they didn't run, you wonder which makes a better shield: an arm or a wall? It depends really, it depends on the details surrounding both.

For the record, because you care, she died on 15 September, twenty years past. The time was 15:33, they were trapped there thirty-seven minutes on the dot.

The mother's name is Fatin and her daughter's name is Rayan. These are facts. The rest is a feast for the dogs.

THE WORDS

It is an old dream, her grandfather dream. They sit together, they stare at the street. They talk quietly, he asks her about school. 'One day,' he says, 'you will no longer live here.'

This single sentence follows her everywhere. He meant it hopeful but she wonders if it is also a curse. She lives in a place, one year, two, and then she moves her place. *The one dispossessed is condemned to endless dreams.* That was her grandfather quoting a writer despite being an illiterate man. The radio, the TV, he had the words of one well read but in all her memories of him, she never saw him carrying a book, she never saw him holding a pen.

Her mother once told her a story of when her grandfather was ten. 'They were filling out official papers and he had never held a pen so they took his fingerprints instead.'

On her birthdays, he would give her notebooks and always a pen. She never thought to ask if he selected the notebooks himself or if he walked into the market and had them recommended to him.

He once asked her if she wrote in them and she lied and said of course. The truth is she stacked the books, she kept the pens in a box and she only used what her parents provided her. She had the intention of writing in those books, she thought up lines, she promised herself she would write them down but she never did. If she wrote, it was in an ordinary book, not the ones he presented to her each year.

'Your grandfather asked if you know how to write. I told him you do but I don't think he believes me. He wants proof of it, he wants to see you write. He sees reading and writing as magic, and you writing is something he wants to see for himself.'

She took her schoolbooks, she sat outside with him. She did her homework where she knew he could see. All the way till she left high school, this was her ritual in the afternoon.

She dreams of him nightly. He speaks more in that land than he did when he was with the living. Lately the dream has taken a turn. He takes a pen and begins writing, she watches over him, asking him the meaning of the lines on the page. He explains to her, he teaches her word after word. She repeats the sounds and she hopes one day they will be hers.

This dream troubles her and she wonders if she is forgetting the meaning of the words. She reassures herself. She still has their sound, they have not left her behind. It is only a dream, nothing more, but when she goes to the collection he gifted her, she finds every book and pen is gone. The next time she sees them is in a dream where he is writing in them her favourite words.

THE DAYS OF PEACE

Ali was from a village in the north. From the day he was born to the day he died, he remembered his parents and what they believed. His entire life they saved to send him to a city school. There he would have advantages he wouldn't have in the village. For example, he would have the benefit of three languages, one of them the language of the world. He would meet people from different circles and everyone knew it was a matter of who you knew. There he would be away from the village boys who did not know what they lacked and therefore did not even bother to dream. This decision, they all agreed, would bring nothing but good.

    He studied, his face in his books night and day. On the bus, over breakfast, a pen was never far from his hand. When they checked his homework, he waited patiently for them to allow him to leave. When they gave him money for school, he put the money away in case he needed it one day. That pile in the drawer, it grew as he finished school, as he went to university, as he made a new group of friends. They lived the life of ease of his parents' dreams. Their fathers wore suits and their mothers had their hair and nails done. They spoke of politics and their powerful friends, they spoke of all the places they had been. On these visits, he watched them, studying them for clues on how a person ought to live. He ate as they ate, he spoke in their tone of being at peace with the world.

When he returned home, his parents asked about his studies, they asked about his friends. They were good, they said hello, and one day he would invite them around to return the favour of being entertained. One day, one day, but he thought of how they lived, of how his parents could not read, of how far his reality was from the dream. He meant to invite them but he never did. The distance was too great, he would create more work for his parents, and besides, his new friends had better things to do.

He sometimes thought of those friends and where they were in the world. He thought of the university and that world he had left behind. He thought of the studies, of this other life he was meant to lead. He thought of how his parents had begged him to continue and how they told him, for all his promise, his life had turned out disappointing. He thought of this and how there was no resolution for such a distance between the future they had envisioned and the one that was reality.

He thought all these things, the thoughts rising up, disappearing, in the rhythm of breathing. He wished he would have told them, he wished they had believed. His nights were troubled by alternatives but his days were ones of peace.

THE NAME

A long time ago, she had forgotten her own name during the war. Her name would appear briefly, sharp and bright as a star, only to be covered again by clouds. She likened it to a fog: a cycle of vagueness and shadows, sudden clarity, and then darkness again.

It had taken her months to remember her name. She had practised the three syllables, rolling them in her mouth, forcing her brain to hook her name. She had begged herself, speaking as if to another person, 'Please hold my name, please hold it as a bird might hold a worm it hopes to eat.'

She had lost so much—they all had—first her car, then her home and then her four boys, tall gentle creatures too delicate for the horrors to come. The boys . . . their names . . . they live now beyond the clouds but she has her name again and she murmurs it nightly to help her sleep.

She sees the others, also victims of a collective dispossession, holding their entire world in their hands. That woman has more than her, a plastic bowl, priceless, a target for thieves or for worse. She wishes to call to the woman, 'You should hide your bowl,' but she fears that if she makes the effort to say the words aloud, she will lose her name to the air. Then how will she coax it to return?

I have my name, I have my name, she chants to herself as she walks. She thinks now of safety during the day and how to hold her name in the night. She dreams of a name-stone, chiselling the letters into its face and then carrying it as an amulet against forgetfulness. No, better a name repeated in silence than a stone in the day where a dark bird might scavenge it away.

She walks this day to the hill where the sun sets. To walk is to survive; to stand still is to lose what little remains. A nameless elder once told her to count the stars, to remember the path at her back so she has the strength for the road ahead, but that wise one, long buried in the sand, knew the weight of a star and yet never understood the infinite worth of a name.

NUMBERS IN THE DARK

Across the border, the herds, they stand in groups, shuffling like a swarm. It is midnight. Far away, a dog barks and a breeze whips the trees. A baby cries in one of the blocks and a silhouetted hand reaches up to flick the light switch. The darkness total. The night adjusts itself, affirms *I am here*.

The roof has been blown off the eastern wing. She will get to it when she has the time. In the meantime, she uses the rooms with a ceiling even if the windows have no glass. A bed sheet is privacy enough. They have been lucky so far with the dry weather. The radio promises rain but there is wind, the sand, thunderous clouds that flash and cackle and pass emptily over their heads.

The latest, she is sixteen, her arms wasted to bone, all knuckles, bumps at her wrist. She says she is sixteen, unable to repeat the words a second time.

She calls out, 'Get the girl a drink and a chair.' If this one is sixteen, then she herself is the great leader.

The man, a businessman his entire life, narrates her strength, pleading that she not be judged on her wrists and fingers. *A meal or two will fix this and she will be full, healthy, she will be ready to work.*

'I believe you,' she says, 'but this girl is younger than my daughter. She will not do.'

The girl cries—hunger, pain, being alive?

He leads her away, still crying, whispering *there will be tea, there will be bread, one day there will be honey too.*

Another day, another dollar. She has a roof over her head still. She has marked the days. Sixteen. At thirty, she will leave. Somewhere, she has a family. There will be someone left. You can't believe every story you hear. The radio, the paper, the television, they lie as all people lie. It is better if their words are lies, better to believe in a lie than what remains of the truth, buried in the rubble.

At thirty days, she will leave. She must. If they are not where she saw them last, she will go to where they might be.

Little stories, big stories. Humans numbered one, two, three, packed onto a truck. Into the dark, they are swallowed by the night, and at dawn: the empty house, the empty street, a town emptied clean like a pocket.

So many of them empty their pockets here. She hears them beyond the bed sheet strung up as a curtain, their fingers fishing among the coins, so that they do not pay more than she deserves, lips quietly counting the coins ten, twenty, thirty. They are honest . . . every one of them . . . exact. Their exactness is a blessing. She counts: sixteen days and at thirty she will go.

That girl means to leave, she knows it. There is the hope that God will protect them another day, that the roof that remains will not collapse in the night. There are so many ways to die here but so few ways to live.

She stands outside in the cold. She has a small bundle in her hands. They say the night is safer but there are hands in the shadows. The day, the night, it is the same. She will leave as she came: in the night, on foot, swallowed, gone forever, and in a day or two, none here will remember her. Another day, another dawn, the world dishing out death, life, disappearance, as her feet count the steps through the night, counting, so she is not eaten forever by the dark.

TRADITIONAL DRESS

Ali didn't mean to hit the tourist, I swear it with my life. No one wakes up thinking they'll hit the person who keeps the roof over their head, no matter the disrespect and however else humans can be unkind.

Everyone knew him to be a reliable man, honest, hardworking, not one to go back on his word. When the bosses had something that needed to be done they gave it to Ali and they could rest knowing it was as good as already done. How many years had we worked side by side? Saleh says thirteen but everyone knows his memory is not one to count on, even when he's not been drinking, but we all agree that this business of hitting the tourist was only a matter of time.

Ali came in that morning with the bag that had his clothes. He had forgotten the holder, the one he wore around his waist for the knife. It wasn't serious. Any one of us could've loaned him a holder and anyway who would notice if one of us did not have a knife at his side? Between the clothes, the head gear, the smoke and lights, music and dance, was anyone going to see that Ali had forgotten a tiny detail, did anyone think leaving out the holder and the knife was going to stop the show from going ahead.

Ali turned his desk inside out. He checked his car God knows how many times. 'I left it in the bag, it should be here, I did not leave it where anyone could touch my stuff.' We told him not to worry, we told him *let us get ready, it is almost our time*, but his mistake was to keep looking so that when we went out, he was upset and anyone could see he wasn't doing fine.

We went through our first performance, the history of it was read out and the audience seemed to smile. We reached for our knives and they gasped—as expected—but Ali kept his hands at his sides. We turned and then the tourist laughed and pointed at Ali. 'That one there is fake. He doesn't even have his knife.'

We continued and went through the standing, the sitting, the praying, life indoors and out beneath the sky, and the tourist kept laughing but it was always at the wrong time. So much I have pushed from my memory but I still remember him saying, 'They're not even real. This has got to be the biggest joke,' and it is then that Ali put his hand to his side as if to reach for his knife. Necessity, they say, is the mother of invention, so in the absence of his weapon, Ali dragged the tourist from his seat and kept on hitting him until he was pleading for his life.

They were eventually separated and Ali was told to clear out his desk that day. I thought he would yell and scream after that episode but he went away like one whose excrement is running down his legs.

Later we found the holder. It was hanging near the stage with a note from the cleaner. *I thought this might belong to someone. If not, I'll go ahead and throw it out.*

Saleh held the holder up over the bin and laughed while we avoided each other's eyes. 'Guess he won't be needing this anymore,' and after that we didn't waste on the incident a single word.

TETHERING THE CAMEL

The day the floor dropped away from his world, Mouad lost faith in God, government and mankind. The world had gone to the dogs and man was well and truly alone. Unable to trust in the big three, including their followers and cheerleaders, Mouad knew to take matters into his own hands.

He inspected his house and declared it safe.

He considered his employment and concluded there was nothing to be done except to attend on time and avoid sticking his head above the line where his bosses would notice he was alive.

He flicked through his relationships and conceded he was stuck with the people around him for life.

All he could control was the camel he owned and so he set about carrying out the plan he had in his mind.

His camel was fed, given water and patted in accordance with advice of the expert kind.

His camel was kept outdoors and a wall was built to make sure that his camel could always be found.

A shelter—indestructible was the promise—was installed to keep a thunderbolt from killing his camel from the sky.

No other animals—pests or otherwise—were permitted to mingle with the camel as Mouad slept soundly inside.

When he emerged one morning and found his camel unable to breathe, he wondered what he had done to deserve this punishment when he had taken every single precaution he could. The camel kicked once more and promptly died and Mouad thought *such is life* and there was the destiny of all creatures, human or otherwise.

The saying goes: trust in God but tether your camel.

REACTOR DREAMS

The reactor would solve their troubles.

Gone would be the blackouts, of waiting hours for hot water so they could wash their hands. Uninterrupted power, a brand-new world out of a dream. They would touch the switch and then there would be light.

They asked themselves if the government could be trusted. So many promises over the years and only an optimist would call the country a wreck, but the dream of power, it went to everyone's head.

The site was marked out between the mountain and the sea, and other than that shadow, it would have no negative impact on their lives, promise to God. It took three years of builders, foreigners of every colour crammed into their town, to help bring the dream to life. Every politician and his dog came to the opening day and the newspapers proclaimed it a new age.

And it was a new age.

Foreigners ran it, polished it till it gleamed in the sunlight and then cleared out as soon as their contracts ended.

The government was questioned: would you say the dream is turning to dust?

No, no, it is a work in progress and we're working our hardest to get it right.

The night the plant rumbled in the belly was the night they began to fear for their lives. They looked at the barbed wire, the metal, and wondered if this was magic of a darker kind.

When it leaked—no one dared use the word—hardly anyone was surprised except the government who sweated through the conference that was televised. Experts were brought in to restore the faith and once again power flowed into their homes and it was said their town was golden when seen from the night sky.

Eventually it was quietly turned off and left alone to gather dust along with the history books of battles past. It was never mentioned again except by the locals as a symbol of failure and foolishness. 'Let your life not be like the reactor. You trust and believe and hope, and in the end, you realise how your trust was unjustified.'

REACTOR, SHE DREAMS

Nightly Jumanah dreams her reactor dreams. Here is how it always begins. It is her first day and she is awestruck by the interplay of light and metal and their unique silvery gleam. She is qualified, she knows, but she is overwhelmed at the effort and energy required to keep it powered and to do so safely.

That is how the dream begins but then it meanders on tangent paths, taking on that particular quality of those possessed in the dream land. There are variations, too many to recall, but always she awakes and she smiles that what she saw in dream belongs as much in reality.

Lately she is troubled by the atoms and how they are struck by the zipping neutrons. This is fission but not as she knows it. Once it was orderly and controlled but now chaos threatens the system. It is not at the danger level yet but she tells her supervisors and they whistle over numbers, they applaud her diligence and respect for lines that separate the dangerous from their orderly world within. 'They're exceeding the buffers, so it's best we rein her in,' and so begins the task of depowering the reactor to stop her from exploding.

She drags her feet in hallways that once were light and now are dull and grim. Is it her imagination or is the process of desertion already beginning? There should have been nine in her team but they stay home and so the shutdown falls to her and another underling. They turn up daily, they never speak, they nod at the orders they are given before scurrying back to their vehicles. She speaks to no one of her dreams, afraid that to voice them is as great a power as prophecy. Images collide in her head and she wonders if this is how a mind finally comes unhinged. The loneliness that has been her shield has become a condemnation and behind its barrier she is suffocating.

The day they announce the shutdown—indefinite, possibly permanent—she is the only one crying. They console her with tissues, a pat on the back. *This is the turn of change and change is always promising*, and she weeps knowing that her reactor is dying and soon it will be dead.

Always she has prided herself on the order of her mind, the neat progression of her thoughts, but she knows the structure has been disrupted. The steadiness has become unbalanced, the reaction disturbed, and as they walk away, so must she too.

She walks away as she was instructed to do. She carries with her every memory of the reactor's interior, she strokes its exterior as one would a loved one's hand. That night she dreams and she arrives as usual, she wanders the corridors and the rooms, inside and out, but as the dream comes to a close, she knows it is time to walk away. First alpha, then omega, her dream has been exhausted and this is the end.

WEEDING: A TWO-PART GUIDE

DRESS

It was a good restaurant, the best in the east. Couples travelled here for a romantic occasion and it was known as a place for an elegant celebration, an evening highlighted against the grey of other days. The trouble was the current system did not discriminate. It gave entry based on who could pay. *While that is good in theory*, M said, *we wish to set a standard about who can step foot in our door.*

To resort to rules and regulations would have been obvious, bringing them a headache of which they would never be free. *There are strategies*—M said—*that can easily get the message across.* They tried putting cards on every table saying they were reserved which allowed them to decide who gained entrance at the door. It was too haphazard and M wanted a system that could be applied equally each time. *The system*, M continued, *should not depend on who is greeting customers at the front and there should be no delay in the decision about who comes in and who will be left outside.* The system needed to be simple, foolproof and send a message to the community about who was going to be allowed in.

They brainstormed, they discussed what other venues had done. They decided unanimously on a dress code.

Cocktail dress. Women's shoulders must be shown.

A man could not bring his woman here unless she was styled in the correct attire of the place. They justified it by saying that the owner was also a designer and his specialty was the dress code they wanted for their restaurant. This deflected the ire of feminists who were defeated by the line *it is simply a matter of fashion and style.*

In one stroke, they increased both the elegance of their clientele and sent a clear message to those whose religion and culture dictated that they keep their shoulders hidden at all times.

TONGUE

To set a standard was to set a bar, to separate the desired from those who were not. *We don't want villagers*—M again—*we don't want riffraff, we only want society's upper echelons.*

It was done simply. Set a language.

We only communicate in the language of the continent and if you don't speak it, we will not be able to provide you service to the standard that you would like.

This one had a caveat. Should a traveller—Nordic, foreign or laden with gold—arrive at their door, they could discreetly make a judgement on the spot. For everyone else, apply the rules clearly stipulated on the door.

EXILE, NO RIGHT OF RETURN

Dalal is leaving. Her world—what she can fit of it—is in the bag at her side.

This entire country, its familiarity, it is as if she is seeing it for the first time. The wall is cracked, the glass is broken, the air rushes in and there is no separation between the interior and the world outside.

She is dropped off: a woman with her practical shoes, carrying no more than her bag.

How is it people manage this with laughter, without dissolving into tears?

Dalal has a list to steady her, ten points to set up her new life. A house, a job, friends, a phone line to the rest of the world, a journal, a pen to detail her thoughts, good coffee for the morning, clothes, sunshine, a lover if time allows. Once she has these in place, she can say her life is normal without lamenting what she has left behind.

The airport is the same. Each time she had left before had been voluntary but this will be the final time.

She hands over her passport, her papers, she makes a point of avoiding his eyes. If there is even a glimmer of kindness, she will throw away her plans and resume what remains if she stays.

She smiles, testing it out.

He ignores her smile, he holds her eye.

He cuts up her papers with scissors, the pieces raining into her hands, but many slip to the floor and are blown away.

'Once you leave, there is no coming back.'

He stamps her passport, points to the gate.

She repeats his words like a sentence handed down and wishes she could burst into tears, beat her chest, faint on demand, but she does none of these things.

She leaves with her bag and no more and in her heart she knows this departure will be the last of its kind.

FREEDOM IN A LIFE

She left him the keys, the house, the child. He and his family could drown in the sea for all she cared.

She had tried to make it work, she had been open to the advice sent her way. She smiled more, complained less, did her hair as they pleased. She sat with his mother, she listened to the endless stories of his stupid father, she entertained his siblings with tea and coffee and fruit and stories throughout the day and night. She had arranged her home as per his mother's instructions so that the clock was locked up and she never knew the time, she drank from a cracked cup while the nice one smiled at her from inside the cupboard, and then there was her favourite dress destroyed from the time his mother demonstrated how to use an iron to eradicate a stubborn line.

She had known it was a disaster from the start. *Be patient, give it time, you may be wrong.* She was not wrong and she cursed Shaitan who had told her to wait. To wait for what exactly? For him to become a new person, for God to come to Earth and make them see the light, for the world to stop operating as it always had?

There was the dream she had as a child and she once told it to her dad. *I had a dream I was in sunshine. I was in a field and it was the happiest day of my life.* He had asked her why she was happy and she shook her head. *I don't know. I think I was just happy to be alive.*

She remembered because there was little else to do during the drive.

She had driven off in his car because they had agreed one was enough and she was free to use his, because *we're married now, what's mine is yours and what's yours is mine,* and this was a line he had exhausted on her head until she became sick of life.

She thought of her books, how she had given them away because *my lovely, you will not have the time.* Nothing but the bare walls and not a single written word to break up the monotony.

She drove through the light, through the darkness, past cliffs and over hills until she lost all concept of time. She drove till she was senseless and the numbers on her watch were bubbles that she could not decipher even if she tried. She drove till she arrived in the future and she stepped out of the car in the middle of a field and she thought *this is the happiness from my dream as a child.*

What was past was past and what lay ahead was entirely hers once again.

THE NEIGHBOUR

New families were moving into their town. A 'wave' was the wording used on the news. It was said that the newcomers were seeking peace and a fresh start to life. Soon the new and the old will live side by side. Harmonious. Don't let any worries cross your mind.

He let no worries cross his mind. He trusted in God, he trusted in their allies, and most of all he trusted in the goodness of people, everyone's innate desire for peace.

You come in peace and you will find here an even greater peace. Face the world with the face you wish to receive.

Those were his father's words, and peace and freedom were lessons he had learned on his father's knee.

Just as the river leaves for the ocean so all humans have their terminus in a place of peace.

His mother had scoffed at that. 'Stop filling his head with that nonsense. Yes, idealism by all means, but never forget life and its practicalities. If you go around acting like a lamb no matter the wolves you meet, your flesh will be stripped and you'll be reduced to the barest bones. Tell me, what will peace do for you when you are out starving on the streets?'

It was an old argument. Many variations on a single theme. Go ahead press repeat.

His mother came in and made the announcement. 'We're getting neighbours next door.' Abu Ayman had gone overseas and his family had followed and their house now stood empty. He had a brother who still checked on it, who had a group around for cards and tea, who could be heard arguing over politics at four in the morning. His father thought to go visit them but his mother made up enough stories about their type that made it clear it was better for him to stay away from the darkness this new type may bring.

THE VOICE OF THE STREET

They said he was the one behind the protest. Mustapha, wife, three kids, had a coffee stand out on the street. Black coffee, no sugar, a separate flask for tea. The same people stopped by day after day and he knew each person by name. Over the years, there were the stories about their families, their work, what was happening in their communities. When no one was buying, he looked out onto the street.

With the years, the traffic had increased and at first he had welcomed the cars. More traffic should have meant more passers-by, except the equation did not work so simply. More space for cars meant the passers-by were squeezed on either side. Where once they had strolled, their pace was now faster and they were occupied with their phones. When he was starting out, he could stand on the street and call out that the coffee was fresh. Now, he stood on the footpath where people were pressed and the horns and music drowned out his voice.

Still he played music. His radio was small and it disturbed no one. He had one cassette he listened to eight to ten times a day, depending on when he packed up. Fairuz, her songs, they were best served with coffee. When he took a day of rest, he would pour his cup and let her voice wash over him. When no one was close, he hummed along with the songs. There was no work, there was no street, there was only the dream she knew how to sing.

Zein told him about the protest before he left for work. 'It will be this Sunday. Maybe for once they will hear what we have to say.'

Mustapha said nothing. His children needed shoes and a performance by Fairuz would be broadcast in the afternoon.

Before he left, Zein said, 'So many protests. Tell me what do they ever achieve?' They both laughed. Whoever he spoke to, on this point they agreed.

He had not intended to go. There was much he had to do. He told himself this as he walked into the square. According to the radio, they expected the turnout to be large. 'They're saying a hundred thousand. We're told the police are prepared.'

He arrived early and watched the people wander in. He recognised those who bought coffee. They said hello, they asked about his family. Crowds gathered around the fountain and he thought *I have not seen this fountain in years.*

They brought flags, they brought banners, they brought signs they had made. They laughed, they sang, he watched strangers holding hands.

So many protests. Tell me what do they ever achieve?

He thought of the streets, how they hurried more but seemed to make less and less. He thought of Fairuz and the broadcast he would miss.

Perhaps they achieve something, perhaps they achieve nothing, but I cannot ignore what I believe.

The day turned ugly. Everyone said they should have known. *People are so frustrated. They do not want their lives to continue as before.*

People ran, people were chased.

The radio later said, 'How could it turn so violent when they said they wanted peace? The blood of innocents has been spilled.'

They discussed this the next day. It was the only conversation on the street. Each person had their theory and he listened to them as he turned the tape and pressed for Fairuz to sing.

Protest after protest and he left his work to stand with the others in the square. Someone suggested he speak for the workers on the street. He rehearsed his words and delivered them carefully and he would never forget how they cheered.

His name? *Mustapha.* Family? *Wife, three kids.* Education? *He stopped school at thirteen.* Employment? *Coffee seller on the street.* Ideology? *We are waiting for information to come in.*

They asked his family, they asked his friends. No one trusted these strangers enough to speak. Even threats had a reverse effect. People shut their doors, they pretended they had never heard of him. But their questions were not futile. They learned a couple of things.

They invited him to the presidential palace. Before him they put a feast. The food looked delicious but he felt only sick. The band played Fairuz and he thought of coffee and his work on the street. They offered him work with them. More money, a better house, his family would be denied nothing. One gestured to the table. 'This is a celebration and now we shall eat.'

He wondered what they were celebrating, what he would be asked for in return for the promises they had made. He opened his mouth and told himself to eat. *A little bread, a little meat, tell me if this changes anything.* They were eating already and he thought about those who begged, the people who hurried more and more, walking straight over the ones stretched out on the ground, their hands held out.

The songs of Fairuz made him look up and he saw that this music had been chosen so he would believe them the same as him. *Once a man of the street. Now your life will be comfort and ease.*

He excused himself, saying it was for a moment, believing he needed a break and that he would come back in, but as he walked away, he knew his choice had been made and now again he could freely breathe.

QUESTIONS WITHOUT A SOUND

Her family made these jokes.

Hiba has so much luggage, the plane won't take off.
What use is a washing machine if there's no electricity?
She says she'll be gone for months but I give it a week.

Contrary to their predictions, the plane did take off and the plane also landed. She paid a man to push the trolleys with her suitcases, she paid another man to deliver the oversized pieces to the house.

Hiba had never been here before but she was determined that this country be her home.

She had the washing machine, fridge, microwave, dishwasher installed in their place. She did not mind that the electricity was cut half the time and the water in the tank ran out each day.

A place does not adapt to a person. The world demands it the other way. This became her line, accompanied by the smile she kept on her face.

She took her coffee to the roof each morning to watch the sun rise. After it rose and once she had emptied her cup, she was watched by the townspeople as she saluted the sun and disappeared into a downward dog. They were familiar with these moves. They saw them practised by westerners in the shows they watched. What they had not seen before was a woman with her breasts hanging free without a bra to hold them in place. They offered advice about this. *Yes, the exercises are good but draw modesty over you like a cloth.*

She ignored them. She had intended simply to move from one country to another. She still believed in living her ordinary life.

When the electricity was cut twice a day, they complained while she applauded returning to traditional ways.

When the men complained that fuel was expensive and the taxis were old and unreliable, she pointed to their feet and said, 'God has given you two feet. What about using those?'

When the women worried they had to wash by hand, Hiba clicked her tongue and said, 'At least you have a pair of hands.'

And she meant this. She did not mind cleaning the dishes and clothes by hand or visiting people on foot, but she wondered if her appliances could really be transplanted from one country to another without being rendered useless.

When her family called to check on her progress, she knew they laughed behind their hands and that they continued with their jokes.

How useful is that washing machine?

Are you enjoying walking because you cannot trust a car to turn up on time?

She laughed with them. Yes, life was one big laugh, but the next morning she called a man and requested his assistance for an hour. Her neighbours gathered to watch her which was how they now started their day. They were surprised when a stranger lined up the washing machine, fridge, microwave and dishwasher on the roof. *Any moment now she will start her routine* they said, one person to the next.

They later called it the not-so-ordinary day, the only break in an otherwise clockwork routine. One by one, the appliances were pushed off the roof and the sound of their crash reverberated through the town.

She paid the man and he left, and they wondered what this meant. They pointed to the heap and formulated questions in their mind. When she walked through the town, they told themselves they would ask but they could only see how her breasts still hung free. That silenced any questions they had about the twisted appliances on the ground. They meant to offer her advice, to caution her, but when they opened their mouths to speak, a look from her and they shut them again without a sound.

THE NEW FRIEND

(A FABLE)

Say you have friends but they're weak friends. Say lately your friends have left you alone, perhaps they haven't been as nice. Or say lately they have been the same but this other friend has caught your eye. Imagine this other friend simply smiles, that they take the time and that is it. Enough! You feel recognised and you realise that this other friend can help you spin a nicer life. You can be cooler, you can be better, you can be tough. Most of all, you can be untouchable. Say you leave your old friends—*it's just this day, promise, I'll be back tomorrow*—to see this new friend. You forget your history with this new friend, how they once tormented you by calling you names, how they set the trend for the taunts of the rest. You forget it because it is in the past, it does not count and now you can be party to the taunts.

Let us not mince words. You accept, you submit, you relent.

It is fun for a while, the new crowd, and if it hurts your old friends, well, so what? They belong to the past and can't everyone see how freely you laugh these days?

You laugh when it's justified. You laugh when it's not. You laugh at how they made you cry, you laugh that you're not as bad as those who make up the chants. You laugh especially at your old friends who look so alone without you, their heads fallen to honour your absence.

You laugh but at night you cry because it is unfair and you don't like who you've become, you cannot stand who you were. You cannot stand it, you cannot bear the memory of how you were pushed around. You cry, you cry delirious, and you pray soon you will forget. One day no one will remember who you were. They will only know to smile at you, as if at a predator, because if they don't do so respectfully, you have this new pack at your back.

THE SUICIDE BOMBER

I am allowed my life.

No, you are not.

After Suzan died, there was the funeral, the coffin paraded in the streets.

There was a surge in the sale of flags.

There was an increase in that year of people naming their daughters after her.

Her poster—the photo unsmiling—haunted the townspeople as they walked the streets. They dreamed of her eyes following them, imploring, *come on, why don't you do more?*

There were more recruits, some unsuccessful, some who walked away at the last minute. Perhaps they were afraid, perhaps they were unsure, perhaps they questioned religiously whether it was even right.

Long after her image had faded, her parents kept a shrine that greeted guests on their way in. Visits from certain guests increased. Others made excuses and after the funeral their faces were never seen again.

Her parents spoke of her still, a young woman as she had been in life. They never mentioned her death and if it weren't for the shrine, one would think them in denial that she had died.

The words said in the house before her parents were not the same words heard on the streets.

She was a strong woman.

> *She should have married
> and had some kids.*

She was a believer.

> *Only those who have rejected God can kill
> innocent people as she did.*

She believed in freedom.

> *If she believed in freedom,
> she would not have killed herself.
> Did she believe this is how we would be free?*

She knew what she thought.

> *She allowed others
> to play with her mind.*

In paradise, Suzan has coffee and speaks to God.

A dialogue is what she wants but she hears no voice and so she concludes that this is a monologue.

How can you allow such suffering?

Why was death my only choice?

I would be alive still if I had a chance at an honest life.

All my education, all my brains, and my end was driving a truck into a stranger's house.

What do you think of the freedom that I chose?

The coffee is endless. It is bitter when in life she liked it sweet.

There are whisperings of a Creator, a Keeper, a Power Above.

There are whisperings. Mainly there is silence.

She drinks her coffee. She has no more questions for once.

She is quiet.

God is quiet.

Someone once said that her choices in life are hers alone.

The only conclusion is that she is alone and more than anything that person is wrong.

GRANDMOTHER SO SICK

When grandmother became so sick, we took her to the hospital. She was scanned and tested, she was asked questions, her symptoms and results were documented and she was allocated a bed in the ward.

She was sick, she was diagnosed, it was expected her recovery would be complete.

They were right. Of course they were right.

Ten days later, we shook hands all round and took grandmother home, and no one could believe she had been so sick.

When grandmother became so sick, we took her to the hospital and we were asked for insurance papers at the door. Lucky we brought them and they took her in and gave her the room she needed so she could begin her recovery.

For the time she was inside I was conscious of how unwell she was, how other people waited outside. I could see them from the window whenever I looked but the nurse shut the blinds and told us it's a policy they had just brought in.

Grandmother made her recovery, thankfully she did. She plays with the kids now and we count it a miracle that she continues to be here.

When grandmother became so sick, we took her to the hospital but we were told that without insurance, we would have to pay because these are difficult times. There aren't enough beds, enough nurses, enough doctors or enough medicine. The sick and paying would be given priority and if their payments came through, allowances could then be made for those who could not afford to pay for health.

We waited in the streets, we waited like everyone else. We put together money for a day and a doctor's cheque and one packet of medicine.

She takes the medicine daily, the most important one from the list. The others are recommended and we will try to get them for her next month if we are still here.

When grandmother became so sick, we took her to the hospital but we were turned away because these are unprecedented times. We wait, we hope, we pray and we remember that for every human God has already written a time.

THE INVASION

When the invasion happened, Khaled was in the living room. His mother was outside and his sister was watching cartoons in the next room. His father was chopping wood and he was meant to be helping but Khaled found himself unable to move.

The news had been warning them for days. The trademark signs were there. The hardline stances, the swooping over the country's airspace, the negotiations that had failed in their latest round.

The invasion was coming and Khaled kept thinking he wouldn't have to go to school. He had been trying to tell his parents that he wanted to drop out, that school was not for him, but they had brushed him away and told him to persist. To persist in what? The crappy grades? He failed everything except maths and, let's be honest, in that subject he was scraping by. Was he to persist because it was their dream, not his, that one of their children would go to university and they'd be able to hold their heads up high in the street?

So when the invasion happened, Khaled took to his bed and tried to ignore the world outside. This invasion had nothing to do with him and now he could make some decisions about his life. He could not go to school so he might as well go to work and that would mean money, some clothes, maybe even a car to impress the girl he liked. He lay in his bed and spun fantasies and thought about the lines he'd say when his father returned, but one look at his father's face and Khaled realised that whether he went to school or not was no longer the biggest problem that he had.

THE ULTRANATIONALISTS

The day the ultranationalists came to march, the animals turned out in the town. There was the atmosphere of a carnival and when the music played, the animals thought the marchers meant to dance.

It started as a dance but when the marchers brought out their weapons, the gazelles knew the dance would become something else. The gazelles could see the hyenas were caught up in the chants, that they silently mouthed them, and it was the belief of the gazelles that the marchers had the right to peacefully express what they believed.

The gazelles knew to leave the streets but the bears were undecided and it was supposed later that the bears did not believe that this was their conflict. *The marchers march, their cause is neither here nor there, us bears are not mentioned, we have nothing to do with this.*

First there was the marching, then the dancing, then blurred lines and suddenly there was fighting. Someone was dragged and beaten and it was not clear if they deserved it or if it was the natural conclusion of the marchers taking to the streets.

The bears left and hid and they wondered *should we have said something earlier? Are we meant to be protesting? Did the gazelles realise what we're only noticing now? It is harmless, they are harmless, it will pass, don't let yourself get worked up.*

The hyenas stood and watched and some clapped and others did not. They said the marchers had a right to their hatred. The rest of them thought *it's someone else's problem and ultimately, in time, this will pass me by.*

TARGETS

Later when Saeed remade himself as a businessman, his line of work led to a subject change whenever it came up. Decent people knew to turn a blind eye and their decency was maintained by staying away. *Silence, Saeed does not exist, the key is to keep our heart and tongues clean, to not forget we will have our end.*

There are others who like to talk, who said Saeed's father had always owned their town. It started in the civil war, as most things did, and the country had not recovered so he kept his stranglehold.

Some things were forgivable and others weren't and there were few arguments about which side of the line Saeed's work fell on.

He schooled them, Saeed did, on the expression of terror, on handing over their papers, their belongings, so he could ensure that they made it to their destination after they'd paid the required sum. *Your papers, you don't need them*, and to demonstrate, he burned them and scattered the ashes once the fire had had its way with their details, their faces, and finally their names. He stamped at the ashes and got a broom and threw them in the garden, and he reminded these people that the less they knew the better and that on the boat there was no space anyway.

And he was right, on the boat there was no space and for hours they were in darkness—fumes, lack of oxygen or light or any food—and they remembered Saeed's words: *trust me, they have to believe you're desperate people on the run.* And they felt it now, that they embodied the story exactly as Saeed had planned and when they were finally rescued, they were penniless strangers who were deported or in need of refuge, and if they could curse Saeed to his face they would, but he was powerful as his dad was powerful and Saeed had money while they did not. And now they were at the mercy of the world and what the tolerance of strangers could provide.

HEELS AT THE PARADE

Really this is the time of troubles. People don't have enough to eat, there is an outbreak of violence and there are more children begging than the schools could ever hold. And again the record is broken and each day it is the same news and the country has gone to the dogs or to hell, which either way equals about the same.

The only highlight is going to the parade and today it is on again but yesterday it was called off but they'll go anyway to stand in the streets and cheer or cry and the last time there was a parade, there was also trouble so if you know what's good for you, it is best to stay away.

But she stands there in heels, made up, hair pinned, smiling, clapping, and acquaintances comment on her shoes, their flashiness, their impracticality, and all she can do is laugh and clap and pretend she can't hear what they say.

This is her first outing in a month and though she's had visitors, she hasn't returned any visits because she has nothing she can put on. It isn't a matter of clothes. No, she has enough clothes. She has enough clothes to give away, she has clothes and nowhere to wear them to, she has clothes she wishes she could barter but not a decent pair of shoes to wear them with unless she goes in bare feet or in these heels. She once had shoes but she lost a pair, lent someone another, had three pairs stolen in a break-in, and now she is left with nothing but her house shoes and these heels. Every day is a party except there have been no parties and she comes out despite the warnings because she has not dared to go out since the last time she was robbed. Instead, she gives money to the kids to get her things, and that way no one knows the truth, that in fact she can't afford another pair of shoes and she hides this by telling the kids to keep the change because she has plenty to give away.

JUGGLING

The child is juggling in the streets and it is something we have seen before. His parents have dressed him in his best clothes but even this outfit has seen better days. His act is better suited to a circus than the city square but each day at this time he comes here and he leaves at the end with a pocketful of coins.

I feel the need to say straight out that I don't support this child juggling, that to give him money is to encourage others like him onto the streets. He is a child and he belongs in a school and if his parents need money, there are programs run by the state. It is deliberate, these worn clothes they dress him in, and they send him here alone, knowing he is more sympathetic if he is seen by himself while they quietly watch from the sides.

We watch. It's hard to miss the act that stops the city, that makes people chat, that makes them laugh, but it just goes to show that people don't have much happening in their heads nowadays. What really does it for me is that he drops the ball and makes the same mistake every day, but the people watching continue to clap anyway.

THE READING

... and she knows as soon as they bring him in that his situation is bad and one look and it's there to be read in his face but she does not despair and she wonders what could be a big enough offering to God to keep him there for a few more days and that is how she picks up the Book and begins to read, starting with the shorter pieces at the back, and these are the words she has recited since childhood but now she reads them differently because she can see he is fading and she is going to make him stay so that is how she reads, uninterrupted, taking a breath at the breaks, thinking it is too early, he is too young, will he even make it through this day because already they are telling her to prepare herself but she refuses and tells them so and they back off because she will allow no doubt and the message is clear on her face, and even when he stops breathing, a minute, two, they're asking her to step outside but she knows if she keeps going he cannot be taken because there is a God who can see she is not ready, neither is he, and *hear me here, I am calling upon Your Grace*, and that night she reads through the darkness and then there is the glimmer of light but he does not move and she knows he never will move again, that this morning he'll be buried, he'll be gone forever, because she has finished the Book and she no longer believes in it, or in life, or in God, or that she'll see him again in the afterlife.

CHOOSE YOUR OWN ADVENTURE

VERSION 1

He had been a businessman these twenty years past. The fuel was his. It had never been this bad, ever.

People were smuggling fuel and it was the only way to make a buck. Of course the fuel arrived along dark channels. There hadn't been legitimate ones for months.

The queue formed in the evening. They were waiting for morning time to be the first supplied when the tanker finally arrived. It was assumed it would arrive but this was hit and miss. In the past week, the fuel had arrived three times. The other four days, he had stood in the trailer and told them, 'People, it is time for you to go home.'

There had been some unpleasantness lately. One person had brought a gun. One person demanded he prove there was no fuel hidden beneath their feet. 'I demand to see your storeroom as well because we know your family have always been liars and thieves.' There had been knives, there had been the army, there had been the police. The army had been apologetic but they told him, 'These are desperate times and whether you own it or not, the fuel will have to be released.'

He had not believed them but this morning there were all the players: the locals, the out-of-towners, the spectators, the army, the police. They demanded he share the fuel, no matter how few litres he had. 'There is no fuel, I swear it to you,' he repeated to them again and again in the summer heat. He repeated it so often that he was dizzy and tired and thinking *really, this is a catastrophe*. He was crying but this did not dispel them. Perhaps they saw it as weakness and thought *we shall move in for the kill*. He fired a few shots—harmless—to get them to take a step back and he wasn't paying attention when the tank of fuel materialised. Honest, he was certain he was shooting where there could be no harm, but a bullet hit the tanker, the flames could be seen from the capital, the explosion was felt three countries away, and everyone thought *this is the latest episode in a situation already very bad*.

VERSION 2

The day was hot.

Why do people fixate on this detail? Is it important? Is it what set off the chain reaction that led to the 182 dead and no one having time to tally the injuries?

Fact: it was over fuel. The army was involved. They confiscated the tanker. The locals butchered each other because they believed there was fuel hidden away.

Someone had a gun. Actually many had guns. A gun, an explosion, et cetera, et cetera.

Lucky for us, no one we knew died but the way things are going around here, let us say that there is still time for that to change.

VERSION 3

This is also likely:

The army arrived to protect a business owner.

There had been extra activity lately involving thieves, highway robbery targeting tissues, fuel. They also lucked out with masks to administer oxygen but never mind the oxygen tanks had been empty for weeks.

There was also a greater army presence on the streets. Those who were cynically minded thought the army was going to install a president, but really, who wanted to be in charge of a mess like this?

And it wasn't only the petrol stations with soldiers posted there for protection. The decree had put the entire army on the ground: supermarkets, hospitals because people were robbing ambulances as they waited to unload patients in emergency.

Dire, yes, but the army presence was understandable.

People didn't go out alone anymore. They moved in packs. They took their guns. The medicine didn't make it through but somehow the bullets always did.

The army was on the left. Yes, just there. The bandits were on the right. They said they were going to take the tanker—full as it was—and the army had better stand to one side.

The army blamed the bandits. You can imagine who the bandits blamed. I have it on good word it was a bystander—well meaning, of course—who accidentally shot the tank.

That is the story that arrives to me but the people able to verify it are actually dead.

BLACKOUTS

It's a story and they'd heard it all before and it was that Rayan's house never had power cuts. Some days the reason went it was because she had a brother at an important power plant and other times it's because their generator was a new one, running on the sun or something, and for this reason its fuel never runs out. There was one version they all loved and it was that her family had so much money that they never sat in the dark, and it was funny, especially the times when Sawsan went past Rayan's house in the night-time and, in one hundred per cent of the house, there wasn't a single light.

AT LAST

At last, the end has arrived and the country has collapsed. The end, this is it, the mood is one of relief.

Consider it. They had been stockpiling fuel, flour and pens. They had enough fuel to get them through the winter but after that their future was well and truly in God's hands. They had medication, antibiotics, pain relief, sanitary products for the women who needed it in the house. Surely the situation had to improve because it couldn't get any worse than its current state. Spare light bulbs, tissues, rice in case the flour ran out. The children said they wouldn't eat rice even if it was the last thing on Earth. Everyone was hoping it wouldn't come to that. There were two spare tyres: one for the truck, one for the car. Not enough, they knew, not when the goods entering the country had been frozen for months. They had negotiated with store owners—*we have eight kids, there are also the grandparents, won't you tell us when the supplies arrive?*

Yes, yes, of course, but if someone comes waving money in these times, who is going to blame the one who thinks of their pocket and their family that needs to be fed?

They make their plans, as people all over the country do, and now they wait and hopefully God comes through like they prayed He always should.

THE SCATTERING

The scattering of this family:
there is the war
the exiles by necessity and then those self-imposed
those that sought their fortune far away
buoyed by hope and a dream
then there are the lovers
the delusional and the regular kind
professing eternity, infinite bonds
for you I lay down my life
and then the children leave
then their parents seeking them
the rebuilding
in the shadow of paradise
it was golden
now the memories begin to fade
what will remain
once death has had her share
and time has scattered the rest
except a name and a tie
a memory of what we once were
once upon a time

exiles from a nostalgia's paradise
remembering   remembering
like dust
the days settle
and us with them
as destiny delivers our hopes
or perhaps she does not
there is the next life, perhaps
we call on God to safekeep eternity
so in the migration we are not lost.

Yumna Kassab is a writer based in Sydney. She studied medical science and neuroscience at university. Her fiction has been listed for prizes including the Victorian Premier's Literary Awards, Queensland Literary Awards, NSW Premier's Literary Awards, The Stella Prize and the Miles Franklin Literary Award.